W9-DFJ-323

"You're writing a novel?" Bassett asked. "That's really impressive, Abbey."

"Why, thank you." I sat up straighter, shooting a look at Sheldon.

"Gosh," Mona Lisa said, "I didn't know you wanted to write."

"Me *either*," said Sheldon. "What's this *novel* about?"

Don's cool green eyes were on me, so I just waved my hand, terribly casual, and said, "Oh, I'm just drawing on my own . . . life experiences." There, I thought, that sounded pretty good.

Wrong. Sheldon burst out laughing. In fact, he was almost slapping his knee, he was laughing so hard. "What experiences?" he chortled. "I can hardly get you out of the house!"

But I fixed him. Mustering a big fake smile, I said, "Of course, I may have to draw on the experiences of those around me too." *That* shut him up.

But Bassett was laughing! "You're funny, Abbey. I think you're great."

So when Crystal turned to me and asked, "What have you decided—will you go out for track or not?" I looked at Sheldon.

"Yes," I said. "I guess I will."

PHILIPPA GREENE MULFORD is the author of several books for young adults, including *If It's Not Funny, Why Am I Laughing?* She lives in Clinton, New York.

QUANTITY SALES

Most Dell books are available at special quantity discounts when purchased in bulk by corporations, organizations, and special-interest groups. Custom imprinting or excerpting can also be done to fit special needs. For details write: Dell Publishing, 666 Fifth Avenue, New York, NY 10103. Attn.: Special Sales Department.

INDIVIDUAL SALES

Are there any Dell books you want but cannot find in your local stores? If so, you can order them directly from us. You can get any Dell book in print. Simply include the book's title, author, and ISBN number if you have it, along with a check or money order (no cash can be accepted) for the full retail price plus $2.00 to cover shipping and handling. Mail to: Dell Readers Service, P.O. Box 5057, Des Plaines, IL 60017.

The World Is
My Eggshell

PHILIPPA GREENE MULFORD

LAUREL-LEAF BOOKS bring together under a single imprint outstanding works of fiction and nonfiction particularly suitable for young adult readers, both in and out of the classroom. Charles F. Reasoner, Professor Emeritus of Children's Literature and Reading, New York University, is consultant to this series.

Published by
Dell Publishing
a division of
The Bantam Doubleday Dell Publishing Group, Inc.
666 Fifth Avenue
New York, New York 10103

Copyright © 1986 by Philippa Greene Mulford

All rights reserved. No part of this book may be reproduced or transmitted in any form or by any means, electronic or mechanical, including photocopying, recording or by any information storage and retrieval system, without the written permission of the Publisher, except where permitted by law. For information address Delacorte Press, New York, New York.

The trademark Laurel-Leaf Library ® is registered in the U.S. Patent and Trademark Office.

ISBN: 0-440-20243-4

RL: 5.4

Reprinted by arrangement with Delacorte Press

Printed in the United States of America

January 1989

10 9 8 7 6 5 4 3 2 1

KRI

For my mother and father and Shep

The World Is
My Eggshell

One

Keeping one eye on the clock, I swabbed down the counter. Only five minutes left of my last night at the Trackside Diner, where I'd filled in for a week for the regular waitress. Part-time jobs were hard to come by, especially for a teenager who had lived in town for only two months. Even so, I was glad this one was ending.

From the corner of my eye, I saw Jerry, the grill man, come out of the back room. We were alone in the diner. He paused in the doorway, holding a box of frozen hamburger patties, and watched as I scrubbed at a particularly stubborn blob of dried gravy.

"Abbey, doll," he called, "why don't you take a load off your feet and have a cup of coffee with me?"

"Oh, that's okay," I said as he walked toward me. "I'm not tired." Still scrubbing, I edged down the length of the counter away from him.

He stopped in front of the coffee urn. Good thing. I had run out of counter. As he filled two cups, he insisted. "Come on, you can sit down for a minute. The place is spotless, and it's the first day of spring. Let's celebrate!" Putting the cups down, he took my arm and led me out from behind the counter and over to a booth.

Once we were sitting across from each other, he asked, "Do I scare you, kid?" Jerry was lean and weathered-looking, though not much older than I. The first night I worked he told me he had a wife and two children and had gotten the ugly scar which ran down the right side of his face in a bar fight. "Maybe a little," I admitted.

"I'm not such a bad guy, you know." He sipped his coffee. "I wish you were sticking around, Abbey. You're a lot easier to get along with than the regular girl." The regular "girl" was fifty if she was a day.

When Jerry reached for my hand, I glanced uneasily at the dimly lit parking lot. *Where was Sheldon?* He had promised to pick me up on time tonight. There was no sign of our beat-up Chevy.

"Abbey?" Jerry's narrow eyes scanned my face as if he was committing my features to memory. "Am I too old for you? I mean, I know you're only seventeen or so, but . . ."

"Sixteen," I told him for the tenth time. "It's not that I don't like you, Jer." I withdrew my hand from his slightly greasy grip. "In fact you're one of the nicest married fathers of two I've ever met, but . . ."

He burst out laughing just as the door opened and fresh air poured over us. "Move it, Ab," my twin brother ordered. "Ma's going to yell if we're late."

In the car Shel eyed me curiously. "What was that little tête-à-tête I just walked in on? Was that guy hitting on you?"

"Not exactly. Don't worry about it, Shel."

He nodded silently. But as he pulled out into traffic, he said, "Well, I for one am glad you're finished at that dive. I wasn't crazy about you working in a greasy spoon."

"Actually the customers were pretty nice to me. If I heard it once, I heard it a hundred times: What's a nice girl like you doing in a dump like this?" I laughed, but Shel was silent. In the passing glow of the streetlights I studied his profile. Like all of us Reillys, he was blond and wiry. He was also the kind of boy girls always looked twice at. But since Dad's death over a year ago, he'd developed an almost constant pucker between his blond brows. It wasn't a frown so much as a look of intense concentration.

We were passing blocks of rowhouses now. Mostly Hispanics and blacks lived in this part of town. A young kid, twelve or thirteen, was walking down the otherwise deserted sidewalk. I smiled at the way he walked—a long, confident stride, followed by a little "pop" on the balls of his feet. He must have spent hours practicing that walk.

A lot of people pretended to be tougher than they were. It was a matter of survival. Like my mother, for instance. She acted as if she could handle it all—raising Shel and me and our little sister without Dad, adjusting to a new job in a new town. She worked in the public relations department of a big corporation in Stamford. It sounded like quite a change from publishing a weekly newspaper with Dad.

My parents had owned the weekly in a little village in Upstate New York. We three kids were born and raised there. For a while after Dad died, Mom tried to run the paper by herself. But last year, in the week before Christmas, she came home and announced she couldn't take it anymore. She couldn't take walking down the same streets, running into the same friends, *living* in the same house without Dad. She said we had to move to survive.

Many times during the past year I have wondered if it's bad to be as close as my mother and father were. When you live and work together, maybe you become too important to each other, too dependent. Our parents were uncommonly happy, and we kids knew it. They were always together, always working. It took five and a half days a week to get the paper out, and early on, the care and feeding of my sister Joyce had fallen to me.

It was hard enough losing Dad, so when Mom insisted we leave virtually everything else that was familiar, it was like another death. In fact I remember hurting so much there were times I thought I *was* dying. But no matter how I tried to reason with my mother, how much I argued and cried, she was adamant. Almost before I knew it, she had found a new job, sold the *Reporter*, rented a house, and moved us to Norwalk, Connecticut.

Shel interrupted my thoughts. "Have you made any friends at school yet?" he asked in the casual tone he used for sensitive subjects.

"No, but I've only been going there for a few weeks."

"I wish Ma had let Gram send you to a private day school, like me," he said. "I think it's easier to get to know people in a small school. Especially when you start in the middle of the year like we did."

"I would never fit in at some snooty girls' school," I told him. "Besides, Mom wasn't worried *I'd* fail my junior year because of dating. Face it, Sheldon, you're the social fly in the family."

"That's *butterfly*, butt breath," he snapped, and I had to smile.

The other reason Mom agreed to let Gram pay Shel's day school tuition was to make her feel better about our not moving in with her. My grandmother lived in Greenwich, on a private beach. We kids wouldn't have minded living with Gram, but Mom said she couldn't accept charity—even from her husband's family.

Money was one of the problems since Dad died. I guess it always had been, really. It was just that when Dad was alive, I didn't remember worrying about it. I knew we couldn't afford the sprawling house we'd grown up in. I'd heard Mom often enough talk about how "house poor" we were. But Dad had fallen in love with that house the minute he'd set eyes on it. It was pretty special because it was situated on three completely private acres on top of a hill overlooking the Mohawk Valley in Upstate New York. There was a spectacular view from every window. I guess you could say my father lived for the present. He didn't worry too much about the future.

I suddenly thought of a fight Shel and I had not long after Dad died. Shel claimed that if Dad had quit working, the way the doctors ordered him to, he would've lived. My father collapsed in the newspaper office one afternoon because of massive hemorrhaging. For years he'd had serious stomach ulcers, but he had refused to slow down, much less get out of the newspaper business. He wanted to be the best editor in the business, and several years in a row the *Reporter* won the National Newspapers Association's Best Small-Town Weekly award. Shel said he'd never forgive Dad for leaving us so soon.

I said I'd never forgive *him* if I ever heard him bad-mouth Dad again.

"Ma's worried about you, too, Abbey," Shel said now.

I sighed. "Why is she worried about me?"

"Because other than this job, which you no longer have, you've barely set foot outside the house, not counting going to school. You're always hanging around the house instead of . . ."

"I feel a responsibility to Joyce. She's too young to come home to an empty . . ."

"Abbey!" Shel's voice was sharp. "That kid has gone to a friend's house every afternoon this week. Joyce is doing fine. *You* are not. You're practically a hermit! It's not natural, Ab, a pretty girl like . . ."

I snorted with sudden laughter. "Pretty is a *grossly* overused word."

He looked at me silently for a moment as we stopped for a red light. "Maybe you're right," he said. "How about 'reasonably attractive'?" He laughed. "Just joking, Ab. Just fooling around. Seriously, you've got to join the world again. Make friends, get involved at school. All you do is sit in your room, mooning around . . ."

"I am not mooning!" I snapped. "I happen to like to read."

"Course even Ma agrees," he went on smugly, "that you've never been as outgoing and popular as I am."

A flicker of anger flared up inside. I turned away from him. It was like pushing a button, I thought—compare me to my twin, I get my back up immediately. Comparisons were definitely odious. And my mother had always compared me to Shel.

Dad never had. Dad seemed to like me the way I was.

I spent the rest of the drive home staring out the window. A few minutes later, Shel turned the car onto the dirt road that led to our rented house.

As the brown-shingled Cape came into view, Sheldon announced cheerfully, "Well, here we are at the little dump on the hill!" This was one of the good things about Sheldon—he had a knack for making light of all the changes.

We walked up the front steps side by side. At the door he slung an arm around me, confiding, "I don't care what anyone says about you, Ab—you're all right."

"Thanks a *lot*, bozo," I said. He laughed as we walked into the house.

Two

I paused in the living room doorway to look at my mother. She had pulled the wing chair up close to the fireplace, where a small fire sputtered weakly. It might be the first day of spring, but it was still damp and chilly out. There was a book in Mom's lap, but she was staring into space.

"Hi." I walked into the room.

You could almost see her rearranging the lines of her face as she looked up. When she smiled, she was still pretty, but it made me sad to see the way her clothes hung on her. "How was your last night at work, Abbey?"

"Not bad. Standing up for five hours sure gets to your feet after a while." I sat down on the couch, putting my feet up on the scarred coffee table. "But it was worth it," I added, emptying my pockets onto the table. "I made a lot in tips tonight."

"Good. Now maybe you'll have time for some fun. That reminds me. Someone called you earlier, a boy with an odd name." She frowned, trying to recall it.

"Was it Packy Cowburn?"

Mom nodded. "Yes, that's it. Who is he?"

"Just a boy in some of my classes. He's asked me once or twice to meet him at a pizza place on the Post Road where kids from school hang out."

"I'm not sure I like the sound of that," Mom said. "If he

wants you to go somewhere with him, tell him to pick you up here."

"Sure, Mom." I stood up and scooped up my tip money. "I hardly know this kid. Don't worry about it."

A half hour later, I'd changed into my yellow Doctor Dentons and settled into the window seat to read. Joyce was hard at work on a book report due the next day. The sound of her pencil scratching across the paper was soothing. I picked up *Green Mansions* and began reading.

Soon reality had faded away—the cramped room Joyce and I shared, the traffic sounds on the parkway that ran by the house. I was lost in the jungle of French Guiana. Rima, the mysterious bird girl, was crying "Abel! Abel!" as she fell from the burning tree, when . . .

The door flew open and Sheldon burst into the room. "Ab, I desperately need a favor! Do you have plans for the car tomorrow night?"

"Why do you want to know?"

"Because Ma said if you don't have anything *special* to do, then I can take the car and . . ."

"Wrong." I sat up straight, bringing my legs down to the floor. "Friday night's supposed to be my night to get the car!"

"You've always got it, Sheldon," Joyce said, accusingly. "Abbey never gets to drive."

"I know, I know." He threw himself across my bed. "The thing is"—he gave me a look from under his blond eyebrows —"I have *got* to have the car tomorrow night. A guy in school said he'd fix me up, but only if I can drive. His old man won't let him take one of their cars. And this girl he's fixing me up with is supposed to be *really* decent too. Her name"—he stared dreamily into space—"is Crystal Glass."

Said I, "You have got to be kidding." Joyce started giggling.

Actually I was about to say "Take the car, I don't need it,"

when he said, "*You* don't need it. Probably all you're going to
do is sit around here, as usual."

I don't know what a dander is, but that certainly got mine
up. Giving him one of my better fake smiles—toothy, like
the models in the magazines, I said, "Tough toenails. Tomorrow is my night to take the car and I want it." Then I bent
my head over the book in my lap, pretending to read . . .
only Shel began making loud sniffing noises. I let it go on
until I couldn't stand it any longer. "*What* are you doing?" I
asked, looking up again.

"There is a very peculiar smell in here." He frowned.
"*Whew!* It smells as if . . ." He stood up and walked over to
Joyce. "It smells as if you've got"—he grabbed her by the
shoulders and began shaking her, making her laugh—"a
whole flock of *barking spiders* in here! Yes!" he yelled, whipping around, pointing at the ceiling. "There they are! A herd
of the deadly barking spider!" Then he made a rude popping
noise from the corner of his mouth and I threw my book at
him.

Instantly Mom was in the doorway. "What is going on up
here?" She looked only at me.

Shel widened his brown eyes. "Nothing, Ma. Abbey just
winged her book at me. For no reason."

"Mom, I was sitting here in the window seat, minding my
own business and—"

She held up a hand. "Please, kids, I've had a long, hard day
at work and I'm not up to dealing with you three. Can't you
try to get along, Abbey?"

"But, Mom," Joyce began, "he—"

"All I wanted," said Shel, "was to switch nights for the car
with her." He hung his head. "And she got all bent out of
shape over it."

Even though I felt like strangling him, I started laughing.
He sounded so *reasonable*. Mom was saying, "I thought I just
finished telling you, Abbey, I don't want you meeting boys.

And there's another problem." She paused, pushing her hair out of her face. "I've got another dinner meeting tomorrow night, and I'd rather not hire a baby-sitter."

"It's all right," I said. "I'll stay with Joyce. Shel can have the car."

As soon as Mom closed her bedroom door, Sheldon leaned back into the room. "There's one more thing, Ab . . ."

Through gritted teeth I growled, "*What?*"

"When are you going to grow up and quit wearing pajamas with feet?"

By the time I had reached the doorway, my twin was safely in his own room at the end of the hall. I closed the door.

"Boy," Joyce said darkly, "talk about growing up, he should. He is such a troublemaker, and he always gets away with it. Can I sit over there with you for a while, Ab?"

"Sure." I moved over to make room in the window seat so she could climb up beside me. As I put an arm around her, the familiar powdery scent of her hair drifted up to me. Joyce had always had a sweet, dusty scent, even as a baby.

Within minutes I could tell from the slow, heavy sound of her breathing that she'd fallen asleep. I sat as still as I could, though my left shoulder was pressed against the cold glass, and stared out at the darkness beyond the window. It was late now. There were no headlights on the parkway.

I studied the small, serious face staring back at me from the black glass. Shel loved it when people complimented him on his looks, but it made me uncomfortable whenever anyone commented on mine. Growing up in a small town, I had become accustomed to being known mainly as Shel Reilly's twin sister. Shel had been the one to claim the spotlight while I had always hovered outside it. He was the one who sparkled. I was the one people depended upon.

"Children?" Mom's soft voice startled me. "Oh, it's just you still up. I was afraid all three of you . . . It's late, Abbey." She held her old rose-colored robe closed with one hand. Without makeup, my mother looked so much younger . . . and sadder. It just about broke my heart sometimes when I caught her with her guard down, when her face showed how she felt—vulnerable, maybe not so capable after all. "You'd better get to bed," she whispered.

"I'm going," I whispered back. "Go on, Mom. You look exhausted." She smiled faintly, blew me a kiss, and closed the door.

The way she'd said "Children?" just now, so hesitantly, had brought back the day a year ago in February. I remembered the way the late afternoon sun had come through the library windows, spilling across the Scrabble board. Joyce and I had been playing for hours, while Shel and Mrs. Chummy, the woman who stayed with us when Mom went to the hospital to sit with Dad, watched a soap opera on television.

The instant Mom walked into the room that afternoon, my eyes met Shel's. From the way she said "Children?" we knew. Even before Mom snatched Joyce up into her arms, Shel and I knew that Dad was gone. Maybe that is one of the things about being fraternal twins—you share an unspoken communication. When Shel ran out of the house, I followed. He ran out back by the bomb shelter.

The house we grew up in was built during the 1950s, at the height of the big bomb scare, and had a bomb shelter. There was no door over the opening and no ladder or stairs to climb down into it, but we kids didn't care—we used it as an underground fort.

When Shel realized I had followed him, he swore at me. He yelled to stay away from him. Then he jumped down into that big, empty cement room. I sat on the earth-covered rise that marked the entrance and listened to my brother down there making noises no human being should listen to another human being making. But I had to stay. If only because I couldn't think of what else to do.

From the time Shel came back up to the light, it seemed he took charge. He helped Mom make the funeral arrangements, called relatives and close friends. It was Shel who went down to the newspaper office to talk to the staff. I stayed home, trying to comfort Joyce and making sure that everyone, especially Mom, ate regularly.

At the funeral it was Shel who spoke about the kind of man our father had been. I remembered his hands gripping the sides of the dais, his face pale but quite beautiful as he looked out at the crowded church. He looked at me when he said, "The thing I loved most about my father was his great zest for life." Mom, sitting beside me, raised her head and smiled.

She told me later that those few words had comforted her, that Dad's zest for life, the way he went after things, was what she had most admired him for.

A tear rolled down the cheek of the girl in the window. I wiped it away, carried Joyce over to her bed, and tucked her in. Then I turned out the lights and got into my own bed. I lay there for a long time with my arms under my head, staring into the dark.

I had often read about kids losing a parent and not being able to cry over it. The writers of the articles said that buried grief was the most dangerous; could cause the worst damage. Well, I thought, half smiling as tears dripped into my ears, no one would ever have to worry that I was burying my grief. I had cried so much in the last thirteen months that Shel had started calling me a lachrymaniac. I didn't think it was even a real word. At least I couldn't find it in our dictionary. I knew what he meant though.

No wonder Mom and Shel worried about me, I thought, rolling over onto my stomach. Why couldn't I cope as well as Shel seemed to?

Three

I had hardly set foot in the mildewed halls of school Friday morning when Packy Cowburn raced up to me. "You never called me back last night!"

"I'm sorry," I said as he fell into step beside me. "I got home late and completely forgot."

"It's all right . . . I guess." He grinned. "But I wanted to tell you what I did to you yesterday."

I stopped in the middle of the hall to give him my full attention. "What did you do to me?"

"Told Mr. DePace you should be an editor of that new literary magazine he's starting." He looked terrifically pleased with himself.

Packy sat in front of me in English and I'd noticed him my first day of school. It would be hard not to notice Packy—he had dark hair, which fell across his forehead but didn't quite cover his pencil-thin eyebrows, a wide grin, and great ears—they were pointed, like an elf's. "I went up to Mr. DePace right after class yesterday and told him Abbey Reilly should definitely be an editor. I also told him how impressed I was with the ending you wrote to *Wuthering Heights*."

I winced, remembering how the class broke up when I read my ending aloud. Our assignment had been to rewrite the ending of a favorite book, but I chose *Wuthering Heights* because it was one of my least favorites. For years I had heard people raving about what a great classic it was, what a tragic love story. I started to read it with high expectations. Readers are always carried away by Heathcliff and his passionate love for Catherine.

Wrong. It really depressed me. That Heathcliff was a terrible man. He devoted his life to trying to make the people around him as miserable as he was. I didn't think losing his beloved Catherine was a good enough excuse for his behavior.

In Emily Brontë's version, Heathcliff goes insane communicating with Catherine's ghost. Nasty and unrepentant to the end, he dies. I rewrote the ending with Catherine's daughter, who is also Heathcliff's daughter-in-law, luring him out onto the moors one night by pretending to be her mother's ghost. She doesn't *intend* for him to fall off the edge of a bluff. But Heathcliff stumbles, falls, and gets smashed to smithereens on the rocks below.

I think maybe if I'd quit there it would've been better. Instead, I gave this ear-splitting rendition of Heathcliff's dying scream, and the entire class went bananas. Even Mr. DePace laughed. It took him ten minutes to restore order.

"Thanks for recommending me, Pack," I said as we reached my locker. "But I can't do it."

"Why not?"

"I don't know a thing about being an editor."

"You can learn, Ab. That's the point of starting this magazine—so the kids who want to can learn something."

I gave him a long look before shutting my locker door. "If there is one thing I hate," I told him, "it's a logical argument."

He grinned. "So it's decided, you'll be an editor. Now"—he hurried on as I opened my mouth to protest—"the *other* reason I called you last night was . . ." He swallowed, making his Adam's apple bob. "Last week you said you had to work both Friday and Saturday night, but this weekend you're not working, right?"

"Right, but . . ."

"Good! Then will you go to a movie with me tonight?" His eyes were so full of hope, I had to look away.

"I can't, Pack. I'm baby-sitting my little sister."

Just then someone called, "Packy! Packy, I need you!" I looked around just in time to see a round girl with wild honey-colored hair racing down the hall toward us. She latched on to Packy's arm, wailing, "You've *got* to help me. You're one of the brains, you're one of the smart kids. Read my ancient history paper for me? I'm supposed to write eight pages and I've only got *five*. I'm totally panicked!"

Sighing, Packy took the sheaf of papers she pushed at him. "Why do pretty girls only want my help with their homework? How come they never come to me for help with their love lives?" he asked, but she'd turned her large blue-green eyes on me.

"Hello, who's this?" she asked, looking me up and down.

"Mona Lisa Roche," Packy said, "meet Abbey Reilly."

"Of course I've noticed you around, but you never say boo. You must live near me, Abbey. I saw you on the bus last month. There were a few days when I couldn't get my mother's car, so I had to take the bus, which almost killed me. The other reason I've noticed you is"—again her eyes swept over me—"you could be a *lot* cuter than you are!"

"*Mona!*" Packy's mouth hung open in horror. "You just insulted Abbey!"

"I didn't mean to." She looked uncertainly from me to Packy. "I didn't mean . . . I just notice that you don't do much to yourself, Abbey."

Packy slapped his forehead, groaning, "I can't believe this girl."

I started laughing, saying, "It's all right. I kind of understand what she's getting at." I'd noticed almost from the day

I started school that I was one of the few girls in the senior
high who didn't wear makeup and who wore basic blue jeans
and oxford cloth shirts to school. Judging from the way most
of them looked, the kids in this school had a lot of money to
spend on clothing and jewelry. It was obvious that Fairfield
County, Connecticut, was far richer than Oneida County,
New York.

"Hey, Cowburn!" A tall, broad-shouldered boy I had noticed in our English class came up to us. "Who's your little
friend?" He draped an arm around my shoulders and smiled,
making his light-blue eyes sparkle. He had the coloring I'd
always wished I had—very dark hair and very light eyes. In
fact, this boy was so good-looking, he made me nervous.

"This is Jack Noon." Packy's tone was curt. "He's a big
deal on campus, captain of the wrestling team. His friends
call him Noonie, but you can call him Jack." Plucking
Noonie's heavy arm off my shoulders, Packy added, "I was
talking to her first, so if you don't mind—but even if you do
. . ." He took my arm. "Come on, Ab. I'll walk you to your
homeroom."

It's funny when you're new—the minute you meet one or
two people they seem to turn up everywhere. That afternoon I slipped into my seat in English and Mona Lisa waved
from the back of the room. She was sitting between Jack
Noon and a girl with long amber-colored hair. One of those
haughty model types with chiseled features—the kind of girl
who scared me to death, actually.

When the bell rang, Mona Lisa came up to me. "Can I give
you a ride home?" she asked. "Riding the bus is *so* gross.
Come on, let me drive you home."

I was just about to say I'd love it when the girl with the
amber hair came up. "I won't need a ride tonight," she told
Mona. "Noonie's taking me home."

Mona widened her eyes slightly, saying, "Oh. Do you really think that's a good idea?"

"No." The girl laughed, flinging her hair back with one hand. "But how else am I going to get home? You've already said you're not staying for track practice this afternoon, so" —she shrugged—"where does that leave me, *chérie?*"

As Mona and I walked down the hall, I asked, "Who was that girl?"

Mona sighed. "That is my childhood next-door neighbor. We grew up on Perry Street, but then her father made a lot of money so they moved up to Birch Hill. She broke up with Jack last week and he is *destroyed* over her. If you ask me, accepting a ride home with him is like encouraging him." She shook her head, adding, "The poor guy."

Suppressing a smile, I asked, "But what's her *name?*"

"Oh, it's Crystal—Crystal Glass. And she may be my friend, but she's a man-killer. What's wrong?" Mona peered at me, furrowing her high, smooth forehead. "What'd I say? You looked worried, Abbey."

"It's nothing. . . . I'm just thinking about something."

Mona Lisa kept up a steady stream of chatter all the way home. She told me she was the youngest of three girls, her older sisters were "total brains," her parents were "fossils," and she was a "change-of-life baby." I wasn't sure what that meant, but she was already telling me how she ran track but wasn't going to practice that afternoon because her mother insisted she keep a dental appointment.

As she turned onto Silverwood Avenue, near my house, she said, "You're in my gym class, too, you know."

"I am?"

"Yep. You know, if you'd look around instead of at your feet all the time, you might notice people. You're shy, aren't you?" Without giving me a chance to answer, she went on, "So I heard Ms. Kehoe trying to recruit you for track. How come you turned her down, especially when she said you're a natural runner?"

"You don't miss much, do you?" I asked, making her laugh. "I had a job after school for a while, and I've also got family responsibilities."

She gave me a piercing look. "That sounds serious. You mind my asking what they are?"

"I take care of my little sister after school because my mother works. My father died about a year ago. . . ."

Mona got that stricken look people always get when you tell them that. I was almost used to it by now. "Oh, you poor kid," she breathed. "You poor, poor kid." She was silent for a moment. Then she said, "Do you realize I am driving along here and I have no idea where you live?"

I had to smile. "It's the first right after the parkway bridge."

As she turned into the dirt road, I said, "Don't go all the way in." Then I added quickly, "The road's in pretty bad shape, Mona. Really. I can walk."

"No problem. I'm not in a big hurry to get home so my mom can drag me down to the dentist." She made a terrible face, sticking her tongue out and squeezing her eyes shut for a second. Then she added, "Besides, I want to see your house."

As the beat-up brown Cape came into view, I turned to her. "Well . . . thanks for the ride." There was a strange expression on her face. Was she staring at the rusty bike lying at the foot of the steps or the falling-down garage with a door that only closed halfway?

"Who," she said breathlessly, "is *that?*"

"That?" I followed the direction of her wide-eyed gaze. "Oh. That's just my brother, Sheldon." He was stretched out on the top step, catching the rays of the spring sun.

"Why didn't you *tell* me you had a brother?"

"I guess because you didn't ask. I told you about my kid sister, but—"

"Bag the kid sister," Mona said, turning back to stare at Shel. "Are we going to sit down here, whispering about him," she whispered, "or are you going to introduce me?"

So I got out of the car and went up the steps. Shel didn't budge until I placed a foot lightly on his stomach. "There's somebody here who wants to meet you."

Clearing his throat loudly, he opened one eye. "Don't bug me, butt breath. I was almost asl—" His other eye popped open as Mona Lisa's high-pitched giggle came up loud and clear. *What was that?*"

"The girl who gave me a ride home from . . ."

In a flash he'd knocked my foot off his stomach and was on his feet, tucking in his shirt and flipping his hair out of his eyes. By the time I got back down to the car, Shel was leaning against the driver's door, introducing himself. After shaking Mona's hand and saying a few words, he excused himself and bounded gracefully up the steps and into the house.

Mona Lisa looked as if she'd been hit over the head. "Thanks again for the ride," I said. "I guess I'll see you in school on Mon—"

She sighed, her blue-green eyes finally focused on me. "You know something, Abbey? I have the feeling you and I are going to be real, *real* good friends."

"I'm glad," I said, and waved as she turned her mother's little red Honda down the driveway.

There is no doubt about it, I thought as I walked up the front steps, Shel makes quite an impression on people. But as I pushed open the front door, I frowned. Now that Mona had met my twin, was I going to go back to being known as his sister?

Four

I never got the chance to tell Shel about meeting his blind date for that night. Every time I knocked on his door, he hollered to buzz off, he was writing a paper. He had a job in an ice cream parlor in Westport three nights a week. That and trying to adjust to a heavier study load than he was used to meant he hit the books every chance he got.

As soon as Mom's ride picked her up, I took a shower, put my hair up in pigtails, and got into my yellow pajamas. Then I settled into the window seat and began reading *Green Mansions*. In no time, reality was replaced by Rima and Abel's world. Their tragedy had become my own. . . .

"Abbey!" Shel's angry voice brought me back to the here and now. "You're crying again, dammit."

I wiped my eyes with the back of my hand. "No, I'm not. It's this book. It's so . . . Hey!" I yelled as he pulled me out of the window seat. "What do you think you're doing?"

"You're sitting around *grieving* again, and I'm not going to let you!" Keeping a firm grip on my arm, he dragged me over to the closet. "The guy who's fixing me up tonight, Don Champion, couldn't get a date, so you can be it. You'll like him, Ab. He's a really . . ."

I yanked my arm out of his grasp. "I'm staying with Joyce tonight," I said just as she walked into the room. She had washed her hair and wound a white bath towel around her small head. It made her look like a topheavy swami. Holding herself stiff, she sat down on the bed and looked at us with obvious interest.

"Oh, yeah—Joyce," said Shel. "I forgot about her."

"Stop worrying about me. Joyce and I are going to have a little TV-and-popcorn party, and . . ."

His face lit up. "That's it!" He snapped his fingers. "We'll have a party here. I'll call Don. Now, you better get dressed."

"Hold it!" I said as he started to leave the room. "I don't *want* a date. Now leave me alone and stop . . ."

"Why don't you want a date?" little Joyce piped up. "Even *I'm* going out, and I'm only in the fifth grade."

Slowly, Shel turned to look at her. "Since when," he asked, "do *you* date?"

"Since Jiggy Graham asked me to go to the square dance at school tomorrow afternoon," she answered in a tone like *so there*.

Sheldon and I looked at each other and started giggling. "Okay, okay," I said hastily, noticing her lower lip poking out in a dangerous way. "We're just fooling around with you, Joyce."

"Look," Shel said, "I don't have time to argue with you, Abbey. You're going to meet Don Champion and that's *it*. Now, get out of those dopey feet things and put on something snappy while I take a shower."

As soon as I heard him close the bathroom door, I got back into the window seat. Not five minutes later, I was interrupted again. The doorbell rang.

"Joyce?" I said, sweetly, "Would you mind . . . ?"

"Don't look at *me!*" She scampered across the room and dove onto her bed. "Nobody's seeing me in my nightgown, boy."

So I had to get up, throw a robe on over my Doctor Dentons, and pad downstairs to the door.

And there on the doorstep was the most thrilling-looking boy I had ever seen. He was tall and dark with tawny skin and green eyes. The collar of his leather jacket was turned up around his face, giving him a faintly dangerous air. I had never, until that moment, believed in love at first sight.

"Is this . . . the Reilly residence?" he asked, uncertainly. "I'm looking for . . . Shel Reilly."

It was only when I realized he was staring at the top of my head that I remembered my pigtails and Doctor Dentons! *Sweet Jesus, Mary, and Joseph*, I thought. *I look like a big yellow rabbit.*

The person standing behind him laughed. Out stepped Crystal Glass.

"Hello there," she said.

I managed to get out a creaky "Hi. I'm Abbey, Shel's sister." Then remembering my appearance, I added, "I'm . . . sick."

The most handsome boy I'd ever seen chuckled. "Yes, you —ah—*look* sick."

Somehow I got myself back upstairs to tell Shel his friends had arrived. He clapped a hand over his eyes. "It's got to be Don and my date. You mean to tell me Don *saw* you like that?" He peeked at me through his fingers, a smile pulling at the corners of his mouth. "You have a *problem*, Ab."

I ran into my room and jumped into bed, pulling the covers up over my head. But he came after me. "Leave me alone!" I sputtered furiously. "I am *never* going down there again. I am never looking that boy in the eye again!"

"Oh, yes, you are!" Shel yanked the covers off me.

"Why do you care what I do?" I asked as an angry tear made its way down my cheek. "Why are you trying to make me more miserable than I already am?"

"You are so stubborn! If it's the last thing I do, *you're* going to join the world again, Abbey. Now, quit arguing and get dressed." He stalked out of the room.

A short time later I stood in front of the mirror and sighed. I had put on a pair of neatly pressed jeans and a pink oxford shirt. "You look nice," Joyce said. "Very all-American. How come you look so down?"

"Because I look so all-American. Did you check out that girl downstairs?"

She nodded solemnly. "She's really pretty, isn't she? Did you see her outfit, Ab?"

"How could I miss it? It's absolutely gorgeous."

Crystal was wearing maroon pegged pants that were skin-tight at the ankle but ballooned out slightly at the thigh, almost like jodhpurs. On anyone else they would probably look ridiculous. But on her they were dynamite. Her high heels were the same shade of maroon as was her big off-the-shoulder shirt. It was a good color against her pale skin and amber hair.

The problem was that I looked like a baby next to her. There was no way someone like Don Champion would so much as glance at me in the same room with a girl like Crystal.

And when I considered how I looked in my Doctor Dentons, it was dubious whether Don would ever look at me again, *period*.

I was halfway down the stairs when I heard the murmur of voices coming from the kitchen. Flattening my body against the wall, I crept down a few steps so I could overhear as much as possible.

". . . even more beautiful than you promised, man," Shel was saying excitedly. "She is something else!"

"Glad you approve," Don said. "Crystal and I go back to our days at Country Day together. When her old man's business had a bad spell, she had to switch back to public school, but we've remained good friends."

He had a beautiful voice—deep but soft. I crept down another step and rested my head against the wall. I could listen to Don talk forever.

"Your little sister's not bad," he said, and I almost toppled headfirst down the stairs.

"She's not my little sister. Abbey and I are twins."

"Really?" Don sounded surprised. "Well, I hope you understand, but . . ." He cleared his throat. "I don't think she's quite my—ah—type. She looks a bit *jeune fille* for me. Bassett Hunter might be more her speed, don't you think, 'ay, Shel?"

Five

I almost flew down the rest of the stairs and into the living room. If you eavesdrop long enough, you're bound to hear something you won't want to. But knowing I'd asked for that didn't make me feel one whit better. I felt as if I'd been stabbed in the heart.

Crystal was curled up in a corner of the brown corduroy couch, poking at a hole in the fabric. "You've got a rip," she told me with a smile.

"I know. That couch has been in tough shape for a while."

"In fact"—she brushed her hair out of her eyes—"you've got quite a few holes here. Why don't you buy a new couch?"

I looked at her, wondering if she was being deliberately rude or just stupid. But then Shel and Don walked into the room. Holding out a hand to Crystal, Don said, "Come on, beautiful. You can keep me company while I pick up some beer."

Crystal looked up at Shel from under her thick lashes. "Aren't you coming with us?"

I swear, I felt sorry for my brother. He looked absolutely gone.

"No, I—uh—I'll stay here with Abbey. We have to . . . organize some hors d'oeuvres." But as soon as the front door had closed on them, Shel began pacing around the room. "Is she decent or what, Ab? I mean, she is _decent_. I can't even believe I'm going out with her, man!" Then he took off for the kitchen . . . with me, one step behind.

Shel stood in the middle of the kitchen, rubbing his hands together. "Okay, now I've got one more favor to ask. Will you call up that little *chiquita* who gave you a ride home today? What was her name—Lolita Bugg?" He snapped his fingers, trying to think of it.

"You mean Mona Lisa Roche?"

"That's it! Here." He tossed me the phone book. "So give her a call, see—"

"But I just *met* her, for crying out loud. It's pretty short notice too. She'll probably be busy, and I don't want to look pushy or—"

"Abbey," he said, sharply, "dial the number. If she turns you down, so what?"

Mona must have been sitting on top of the phone. She picked it up halfway through the first ring. "Hullo?" Her small, high-pitched voice was breathless.

"Mona? This is Abbey . . . Abbey Reilly."

"Oh, hi!" she said brightly. "What'd you think? That I'd forget you since this afternoon?"

"I'm calling because my brother Shel and I were thinking about maybe having a little party tonight, and—"

"Your *brother's* going to be there? That gorgeous *blond's* going to be there?"

"Uh, yes, I believe that's what I just—"

"You're saving my life! I thought I was going to *die* of boredom. I'll be right there, Abbey. Just give me time to wash and blow-dry my hair, put on fresh makeup, change my—"

"Mona, that will take until tomorrow morning!" I laughed. "Just come the way you are. This is no big deal, honest."

There was a pause. Then she said, "Abbey, any time boys

are involved, it is a very big deal. Now, don't move—I'll be right over!"

As soon as I hung up, Shel asked, "She coming?" I nodded. "Hey, thanks. What would I do without you, right?" He grabbed the phone book and began flipping through it. "Now all I have to do is get Bassett over here. We've got to have an equal number of guys and girls, right, Ab?"

A few minutes later, Shel finished talking to this Bassett person and hung up the phone. "All set. You'll like him, Ab. He's a really nice guy." He opened the refrigerator door and began rummaging around while I pulled myself up onto the counter to watch.

Don't ask me why I asked the question when I already knew the answer. It was like poking a painful bruise to see if it still hurts. "Hey, Shel?"

"Yeah?" His voice was muffled by the depths of the refrigerator. Out came a bar of cream cheese, a bottle of chutney, and finally Sheldon.

"Well, if Crystal is your date, and Don is mine . . . then Bassett must be for Mona Lisa, right?"

Without quite meeting my eye, he took the plate I handed him. "This isn't exactly a *dating* situation here, Ab." He unwrapped the cream cheese and plopped it onto the plate. "It's not that *structured*, y'see." Dumping the chutney over the cheese, he glanced over his shoulder at me. "But I . . . I think maybe Don goes for the more sophisticated type, you know what I mean?" he said gently.

I nodded silently and stared down at my sneakers as he banged cupboard doors, looking for things. "You know something, Ab?" I looked up as he emptied a box of crackers into a basket. "You might consider acting and maybe looking more your age . . . you know?"

"How are you supposed to look and act at sixteen?" I asked. "I'd really like to know. I haven't been able to figure it out."

"Well . . ." He shrugged. "Maybe you could watch Crystal. Maybe you could try"—he made circles in the air with his hands—"imitating her or something."

But then the doorbell rang, and forgetting everything he had just said, I leapt off the counter and sprinted for the front door. Unfortunately Shel got there first and hipchecked me into the wall. Smoothing back his hair, he opened the door.

"Why, Shel." Mona Lisa lowered her luminous eyes. "I didn't know *you* were going to be home tonight."

"Hey, come on in!" He stood aside, adding, "You're looking wicked tonight, Lo—" I cleared my throat loudly and he shut his mouth, giving her a big smile.

Without taking her eyes off my brother, Mona said, "Hi, Abbey. How are you?"

She walked ahead of us through the hall, so I was able to nudge Sheldon and whisper, "Read my lips. The name is Mona. Mo-na Li-sa." He broke up.

In the living room, I told her, "You do look nice tonight." She had on a straight denim skirt, which was slit halfway up her thigh, and a creamy, full-sleeved blouse. Her hair shone softly.

"Thanks." She sounded pleased. "You do too."

The minute Mona sat down on the couch and I took the wing chair across from her, the doorbell rang again. "I'll get it!" I yelled, so loudly Mona and Shel looked startled. "You two stay here and get to know one another while I—"

"Are you all *right?*" Mona popped up off the couch as I fell over an ottoman.

"Fine," I said, getting up. "Just fine." Then I headed for the front door. Here was my chance to make a better impression on Don. Lowering my eyes the way Mona had, I opened the door. "Oh, *hi,* Don," I breathed.

"I'm not Don, but I'll bet you're Abbey," a voice said, and I looked up into the eyeglasses of a total stranger. "I'm Bob

Hunter, but everyone calls me Bassett." He stuck out his
hand and I shook it, returning his smile. I liked him immediately. He had close-cropped brown hair, and his pale-blue
eyes behind their thick lenses were soulful, like a . . .

Just then I heard voices. Peering around Bassett, I spied
Don Champion strolling up the front steps. A case of beer
was balanced on one arm, Crystal Glass hung off the other.
"Hi there, Abigail!" he called. "Bassett, my man!" He
slapped Bassett on the back. "You know Crystal, don't you?
And did you meet little Abigail here?"

"Actually," I murmured, "my name is Abernathy. Abbey
for short." But Don and Crystal had already disappeared
into the living room.

"Abernathy," Bassett repeated. "I like that. How'd you get
such an unusual name?"

"It's my mother's maiden name," I told him. "The only
problem is, people get it wrong all the time."

Bassett and I entered the living room just as Don put the
case of beer down on the coffee table. "Well, well, Reilly," he
said, staring at Mona Lisa, "you didn't tell me you were
going to introduce me to such a foxy little lady tonight."

Don eased himself down onto the couch beside Mona as
Shel asked Crystal, "Can I offer you something to drink? A
beer, perhaps?" Very suave.

"Oh, I'd rather have . . . let's see . . ." She tapped a perfectly manicured nail against her cheek. "I'll have a . . .
mart. Yes, a mart would be divine."

"A *mart?*" I blurted out. "I've never heard a martini called
that before. I think that's what she means, Shel."

There was a moment of silence. Then he said, "Yeah, Ab, I
figured that out."

Bassett touched my arm. "Would you like a beer?" I shook
my head and hurried after Sheldon, who was heading for the
kitchen.

"You can't serve kids *liquor!*" I gasped as he took bottles out of a cabinet and lined them up on the counter. "Dad will—" I stopped myself. "Mom will be furious, and you know it, Sheldon!"

"Look, I'm trying to fit in here, can't you see that?" He went on setting up a bar. "If Crystal wants a mart, I'm going to make her one." The only problem is"—he stared thoughtfully at an empty glass—"I'm not positive I know *how*."

He looked at me. I shrugged. "Gin and vermouth, I think," I said.

"Of course," he said coolly, "I knew that." Then he filled the glass with ice. "Okay, gin." He poured the glass half full. "And a little"—he glanced at me—"vermouth. There!"

In the living room Shel presented the martini to Crystal. We all watched as she took a sip—and her face went funny. "I must've made it wrong," Shel said. "Here, I'll get you another." He grabbed for the glass.

"No . . . no, really," she gasped, trying to smile in spite of her watering eyes. "It's all right. I shouldn't drink anyway. I'm in training."

Perching on the arm of the couch, Shel asked in a reverent tone, "What are you training for, Crystal?"

"Track. I happen to be one of our team's best runners, and I'm determined to duplicate the winning streak I had last year."

"I really admire athletic women," said Don.

"Me too. Definitely," said Sheldon.

"Mona's also on my team," Crystal said. "Aren't you?"

Crossing one leg over the other, Mona nodded. "Umm, hmm. But guess what? I am not, never have been, on a winning streak. In fact I *despise* running."

"Then why do you do it?" I asked.

"Because Crystal convinced me it would look good on my college applications. I have to win a scholarship if I want to go to college." She paused. "Both my sisters did," she added glumly.

"Are *you* going out for track?" Crystal asked. It took me a second to realize she was speaking to me. "Mona told me Ms. Kehoe tried to recruit you, Abbey."

"No kidding!" my twin said. "How come you didn't mention that around here, Ab?" Before I could reply, he turned back to Crystal. "I'm sure she won't go out for it. Abbey hates to compete. When we were kids, my Dad used to organize little contests between me and Abbey. He used to make us race, and she beat me almost every time. It's a shame she's so uncompetitive." He shook his head.

Oh, yeah? I thought, glaring at him, but he was so busy smiling at Crystal he didn't notice. Bassett touched my elbow. "Now will you have a beer?" he asked.

"Oh, my sister doesn't drink," Sheldon informed everyone. "Abbey's something of a straight arrow, I'm afraid."

That did it. In my most sophisticated tone I said to Bassett, "Thank you. I would love a beer."

As he opened a beer for me, I noticed that Don had twisted one of Mona Lisa's shining curls around his finger and was murmuring in her ear, "You've got beautiful hair, little girl."

"What else do you do?" Shel asked Crystal.

"Oh, I'm rather musical," she answered modestly. "I play the piano and the guitar, and I—"

"The *guitar,*" Shel repeated. "Hey, isn't that something? I play it too! We have a lot in common, you know? What's your favorite kind of music, Crystal?"

"Jazz."

Shaking his head, Shel said, "I can't get over it. I just can't get over how much in common we have. Jazz is my favorite too!"

That sent my mouthful of beer down the wrong pipe. "Are you all right?" Bassett asked, patting me on the back.

"Fine," I managed as Shel and Crystal got up and went over to the stereo.

"Do you have any jazz, Shel?" Bassett called.

"Sure, I've got jazz. Certainly, I have jazz. Heck, I practically *collect* it!"

Since when? I thought. Unless he was referring to some old 78's of Dad's. Bassett went over to check out the jazz collection, and I noticed Don and Mona again. They were staring into each other's eyes.

Until Crystal sat down on the other side of Don. He stretched his free arm around her, saying, "Ah, heaven. Surrounded by beautiful women."

I must have tipped the beer can too far, because beer suddenly spurted out of the can, up my nose, and down the front of my shirt.

Crystal jumped up. "Quick! Where are the paper towels?"

"It's okay," I gasped, getting to my feet. "I'll . . . I'll be right back." I turned and stumbled out of the room.

Upstairs, Joyce asked, "What's wrong? Why're you crying?"

"Because," I sobbed, "I am madly in love with a boy down there and"—I gulped—"I just made a complete fool of myself, that's all." I sank down onto the bed, adding, "I know it's not the end of the world. It just feels like it. Oh, Joyce, why am I so hopeless?"

She patted my shoulder. "You're still my favorite sister, Ab, no matter what."

I looked at her. She was grinning. "I'm your only sister, Joyce."

"I want you to see this old picture I found of you and Dad." She went over to the window seat, where she'd been going through the old cookie tin we kept photos in.

The photograph was taken on Gram's beach when I was about twelve. I was standing between Dad and Shel, holding up the four-pound bluefish I'd caught single-handedly. Shel had a hand on my shoulder and was smiling almost as proudly as I was. It brought fresh tears to my eyes—we looked so young, so alike, with the same grins, the same skinny legs with knobby knees.

Suddenly I wished with all my heart that I could go back to the time when the world was my oyster—when Dad was alive and Shel and I were friends, equals. It seemed to me now that everything had changed between Shel and me not long after the photo was taken. He grew up and away . . . and I had stopped trying to keep up.

But most of all, I wished I could go back to the time when I didn't know anything. When I didn't know that people go away, never to return.

A knock on the door made me look up. Mona Lisa was standing in the doorway. "Are you okay?" she asked softly. "Hi," she said to Joyce, "I'm Mona Lisa Roche."

"I'm Joyce," said Joyce, looking up at her admiringly.

"Aren't you coming back down, Abbey?"

I sniffed. "I guess so . . . but I have to change my shirt." As I went over to the closet, Joyce showed Mona the old photograph.

"You know something?" Mona asked, looking at the photo, then at me. "When you were that blond, you and Shel *looked* like twins." She studied me as I buttoned up a clean shirt. "We ought to streak your hair, you know that?"

"Why? You really think it would make me look better?"

She nodded. "It'd also be fun. We could do it tomorrow morning. My mom has a beauty salon in the back of our house. I could do a whole makeover on you! That's one of my schemes to help support myself during college, running a little salon for the kids in my dorm. My mother's teaching me. Come on, let me practice on you!"

"I don't know," I said as we started down the stairs. "I'm not sure I believe in all that stuff. You know, *working* to make yourself attractive to the opposite sex. It's not very liberated."

"Hey, I'm pretty liberated myself, don't misunderstand.

But there's nothing wrong with looking your best, Abbey. Please?"

We were just about to walk into the living room when I heard Crystal Glass say, "I can't get over how completely different your sister is from you, Shel. You're so *dynamic*."

Turning to Mona, I said, "Where do you live and what time should I be there?"

As I sat down in the wing chair again (this time tucking my legs up under me, terribly feminine, like Crystal), Don said, "So, Reilly, you think you want to go out for lacrosse, hunh? Well, if I talk to Coach about it, he'll probably let you on the team even though the season's started."

Bassett nodded. "We could use you, Shel. We lost two of our best guys in the game against Mahopac last weekend."

"Man, I'd really appreciate it if you'd speak to the coach," Shel told Don. "I really want to play."

"But I thought Dad always said lacrosse was as tough as football, Shel, and you never played football at home because you don't have the build for . . ." My voice trailed off. Sheldon looked as if he wanted to strangle me.

"There's less competition in a small private school," Don drawled. "Besides, I *am* the captain. That ought to count for something with Coach, wouldn't you say?" He looked around at everyone. "I'm sure I can get you on, Reilly."

Just then a new record dropped onto the turntable and Crystal held up a hand. "All right, Donny, whose music is this? You'd better recognize it—we heard him play at the concert at Hunter College last spring. I'll be mad at you . . ."

Don nodded his handsome head. "Ah, yes, sweetheart. Give me a minute." He closed his eyes. "It's Brubeck, isn't it?" He looked at Crystal, who made a happy sound.

"O-oh, Brubeck. Of course," said Shel, nodding knowingly. "One of my favorites."

"Are you familiar with Brubeck's music?" Don asked Mona.

Her eyes darted from Don to Crystal. "Uhm, really. His technique is quite . . . superb."

"How about you, Abbey?" Bassett asked, and I thought I saw a faint twinkle behind his thick lenses. "What do you think of Brubeck?"

"I've never even *heard* of him. Who is he?"

"You," my twin asked, "never heard of *Dave Brubeck?* Jeesh, Ab."

"He's an old-time jazz musician," Bassett said kindly, but I barely heard him. I suddenly *hated* Sheldon. Crossing my arms over my chest, I tuned all of them out, all their talk about so and so's technique, so and so's music.

Soon I was in a daydream, a dream of revenge, really. Some afternoon when Shel was playing his guitar, I should sneak Crystal and Mona into the house. I should pick an afternoon when he is also singing one of the songs he writes. I happened to overhear one just the other day (mainly because I was lying outside his room with my ear pressed to the crack under his closed door).

As far as I could tell, Shel's latest song was a takeoff on that old song "Ode to Billy Joe," the one about two kids throwing something off the Tallahatchie Bridge. In Shel's song, a seventeen-year-old girl discovers she's pregnant, and one stormy night decides to end it all by jumping off a bridge. But once she's up there with the wind and rain and everything, she has a mystic vision of her and her child going through life together, so she decides not to jump after all.

Actually, the song wasn't bad until Shel got to the lines:

> O, Maryann, poor unwed mother, Maryann,
> Saved by a vision of her unborn little man.

and I just got blooming *hysterical.* Unfortunately, I got hysterical out loud, and Shel almost knocked my head off when he threw open his door.

"Abbey?" Mona Lisa was smiling at me. "You just laughed. What are you thinking about?"

Everyone was looking at me as if I'd lost my marbles. "Oh, nothing . . . nothing," I mumbled, turning fiery red.

Crystal looked at Shel, asking, "Is she always like this? A little out of it?"

I had a sudden brainstorm. "Actually," I said, before Shel could speak, "I was picturing a scene from my . . . er . . . novel."

"You're writing a novel?" Bassett asked. "That's really impressive, Abbey."

"Why, thank you." I sat up straighter, shooting a look at Sheldon.

"Gosh," Mona Lisa said, "I didn't know you wanted to write."

"Me *either,*" said Sheldon. "What's this *novel* about?"

Don's cool green eyes were on me, so I waved my hand, terribly casual, and said, "Oh, I'm just drawing on my own . . . life experiences." There, I thought, that sounded pretty good.

Wrong. Sheldon burst out laughing. In fact, he was almost slapping his knee, he was laughing so hard. "What experiences?" he chortled. "I can hardly get you out of the house!"

But I fixed him. Mustering a big fake smile, I said, "Of course I may have to draw on the experiences of those around me too." *That* shut him up.

But Bassett was laughing! "You're funny, Abbey. I think you're great."

So when Crystal turned to me and asked, "What have you decided—will you go out for track or not?" I looked at Sheldon.

"Yes," I said. "I guess I will."

Six

Saturday morning I made sure I was the first one up. I had to be if I was going to get the car before Shel did. I had decided to drive over to Gram's before going up to Crystal's for my makeover. Mona and I had told her of our plan the night before, and she had insisted we do it at her house, arguing that Mona's mother's salon would be a madhouse on Saturday.

As I rinsed out my cereal bowl, Shel came into the kitchen. "Hi," I said.

He sank into a chair. "Me and my big mouth." He put his head in his hands.

"What's wrong with you? You look sick."

"I *feel* sick. I raved on about how I want to play lacrosse last night because Don was bragging about how good he was, and I didn't want to look bad in front of Crystal. I never thought for a second there was any chance I could actually get on the team. But good old Don's going to arrange it for me." He lifted his head and looked at me. "How," he asked miserably, "am I going to play lacrosse, work part-time, write for the school paper, *and* keep my marks up?"

"It's impossible to do all of that."

"No," he said, "it's just impossible to do all of it well."

"So eliminate something, Shel." His eyes were puffy and

he really looked upset. I wasn't used to seeing my twin looking anything but confident and optimistic.

"I can't cut anything out. I've already thought about it." Smoothing down his hair, he tried to muster a smile. But the intense pucker was there between his eyebrows. "Remember what Dad always said, Ab. 'You can do anything you put your mind to.' He told me that so often, it irritated the heck out of me after a while. Dad really pushed me. He never pushed you the way he did me."

"Don't you criticize him!" I snatched the car keys off the hook by the back door. Turning back to my twin, I said, "And you're mixing something up."

"What's that?"

"Dad said you can do *anything* you put your mind to. Not *everything*, Sheldon. There's a difference." Then I turned on my heel and left.

Gram was standing in the front doorway, waiting to greet me. "I'm so glad to see you, darling. Not just because the flower beds need to be cleaned out, either. Come in and tell me what you've been up to."

I followed her into the living room, which looked out over the sea. Sitting down on the dove-colored love seat, she patted the cushion beside her. "Have you made any friends yet, and what's Shel up to?"

I pushed away a flash of annoyance and sat down next to her. Then I told her about the party Shel had organized the night before. "Oh, that brother of yours! He's always been so popular, hasn't he? So outgoing. What about school activities, darling?"

"I've pretty much decided to run track, and Shel's going out for lacrosse."

Gram's eyebrows went up. "He doesn't have the build for that, does he? All of you children have your mother's delicate frame. Now, your father—Rob was a big, strong kid always.

He was a star, a three-letter man, in college, you know." Her blue eyes got that deep look they always got when she talked about Dad, her only child. "I remember I didn't want him to play so many sports in high school."

"Well, I don't think Mom's going to be happy about Shel going out for lacrosse. I know she's going to worry he'll get hurt."

Gram smiled. "That wasn't what worried me about your father. No, I was afraid he wouldn't be accepted by his father's alma mater. But he was."

I frowned. "I thought Dad went to the state university."

"He did," Gram said. "And I thought it would break his father's heart. Oh, they had a fierce competition, those two. Rob, your dad, reacted to it by doing the opposite of what his father had done. Just to spite him."

I nodded, having heard Mom talk about Dad and my grandfather over the years. "That's why Dad bought the *Reporter*, right, Gram, instead of staying with the family paper in New York?"

"That's right. And what a row there was over that announcement."

"Did Dad . . . did he *ever* do what my grandfather wanted him to?"

"Not very often, darling. Your father had a will of steel, just like his father, which was, of course, the crux of the problem."

When Gram went out to the kitchen to make some tea, I went outdoors and got to work—if clearing out a sun-warmed garden on a perfect spring day can be called work. In what seemed like no time, I was done. I was standing by the seawall, listening to gulls calling to one another as they wheeled overhead, and watching waves break gently against the sand when Gram called me. I turned to see her heading toward me, carrying a wicker picnic basket.

We sat on the stone wall and dangled our legs over the side

like two teenagers instead of a grandmother and grand-
daughter. I kept sneaking looks at her, wondering how far
past seventy she was. She'd had almost no trouble sitting
down on the wall, the way some older people might have.
"Gram," I said, "when someone says you're *jeune fille*, it's not
meant as a compliment, is it?"

"I wouldn't mind being called that at my age." She sighed
before turning to look at me. "After all, Abbey, you *are* a
young girl."

"I know." I looked away, not wanting her to see how
much it had hurt. "But the problem is . . . it was said by a
boy who's a friend of Shel's. It wasn't meant as a compliment, was it?"

After a moment she said, "No, I suppose not." And I ap-
preciated her not trying to talk me out of my hurt feelings.
"But if it bothers you, darling, why don't you change the
way you look?"

"I've been thinking about it, but . . . The thing is, Gram,
you're one of the most liberated women I know. Do you
think it's liberated to wear makeup and all that, just to be
attractive to men?"

She looked pretty taken aback. "I do ten minutes of exer-
cise most mornings and spend quite some time after that
fixing myself up, even though my husband has been dead for
fifteen years. Does that mean I'm trying to attract another
man?"

She looked so indignant, I burst out laughing. "No, of
course not. I guess you have to stay in shape. I mean, you
still go into town once a week for those committee meetings
at the paper."

She looked slightly mollified. "Well, there's nothing wrong
with wanting to look more grown up, Abbey. Don't be
afraid to experiment a little."

"I knew you'd give me good advice, Gram." Meanwhile, I

was thinking—*jeune fille*, my foot! I'll show that Don Champion . . . and Sheldon too.

An hour later I pulled up in front of the house just as Shel and Crystal came out the door. She was wearing a navy blue sweat suit. Her long hair was tucked up under a bright yellow baseball cap, which was turned sideways. She looked great.

"Hi there!" she called as I got out of the car. "I came over to pick you up. Get some sweats on and we'll run up to my house. You might as well start training right away." She smiled at Shel.

"Good thing you got here when you did, Ab." He grabbed the keys out of my hand. "I've got to get up to school. Don called. He's already spoken to Coach for me. I'm in like Flynn, man." He gave me a jaunty grin as he got into the car. There was no trace of the uncertainty he'd shown earlier. "See you later, baby," he called to Crystal as he peeled out of the driveway.

"Did you know," she asked, following me back up the steps to the house, "that your brother has asked me out for tonight?"

"No."

"Well, he has. And Don and Mona Lisa are doubling with us. Isn't that great?"

"Terrific," I said, and went upstairs to change. Crystal followed me, happily chattering about everyone's plans for that evening.

As I changed into gray sweat pants I decided that I was a terrible person. I mean, it wasn't Mona's fault that Don was attracted to her. And it wasn't my twin's fault that I resented him for being so *good* at everything.

Ten minutes later Crystal and I were jogging, side by side, up Silverwood Avenue. Out of the blue she said, "My father was supposed to come home today. He had planned on going to the meet tomorrow to watch me, but we got a call this morning. He can't make it. For a change." She gave an unhappy laugh.

I glanced at her. She was running easily, while I was already winded. "That's too bad . . . about your father. Do you mind if we walk awhile?" Without waiting for her reply, I slowed down. "What does your father do that he's gone so much?"

"He promotes new products—new inventions I guess you could say. He's been on the West Coast for six weeks trying to sell a new treatment for rabies to a drug company. He's gone bankrupt twice." She was looking straight ahead.

"That must have been pretty hard on you and your mother."

She nodded, glancing at me quickly. "I don't know how she stands it. Waiting for him, I mean. She spends half her life waiting for my father to come home. It's like not being married . . . not having a father."

"Your mother must really love him," I said. "You're lucky."

Crystal gave me a look, almost scornful. "I don't believe in romantic love, certainly not between people who have been married as long as my parents have." Then she smiled slightly, adding, "You really are a very little girl, aren't you, Abbey?"

Instead of answering, I began running again. She was wrong about love. I knew. I had memories of my parents' marriage to prove she was wrong. The sound of our footfalls and the whoosh of passing cars faded as I remembered the last summer my father was alive.

We had just arrived at Gram's for our two weeks. Every summer it was the same—we'd pile out of the car and race down to the beach to greet it, reacquaint ourselves with it almost as if the sand and water were old friends who had missed us.

I remembered walking up the beach with my parents while Joyce and Shel examined something by the water's edge. The sun was slipping into the sea, tingeing everything with violet and gold. Mom and I had gone some distance before we realized Dad had stopped to look at something in the sand. He stood up, finally, and held it out to my mother. I remembered the expression on her face as she turned whatever it was over in her hands. Then she looked at him, murmuring, "Oh, my sweetheart," and threw her arms around his neck.

The emotion in her voice was so intense, so pure, I was embarrassed, as if I had seen something that was none of my business. I ran to join my brother and sister, leaving Mom and Dad to walk slowly up the beach, their arms wound around one another.

Later that night I found myself alone with my mother for a moment, so I asked what Dad had given to her. Out of her pocket she took a gray heart-shaped rock.

"Abbey?" I turned. Crystal had stopped at the corner while I'd run across the street. "What were you thinking about?" she asked as I walked back toward her. "If I hadn't stopped you, you might have gone on for miles."

I nodded, mustering a smile. But I was thinking, *Maybe I should forget all the things that will never come again.* What was the point to going back to a time when life was perfect? The world had been my oyster and I hadn't realized it. When my father died, my world cracked like an eggshell.

I closed my eyes tight against the wave of grief that swept over me. Even after thirteen months, grief, palpable like pain, still came, reminding me that everything had changed. Nothing would ever be the same.

"About time, you guys!"

I opened my eyes to see Mona Lisa waving from the front porch of a gray house with white gingerbread trim. It was one of the prettiest houses I'd ever seen. To the right of the front door was a magnificent stained-glass window with a purple and blue iris design. "I've been waiting for close to half an hour," Mona called as we crossed the lawn toward her. She held up a brown paper bag. "Here's the streaking kit. Your mom went out to lunch, Crystal. She said to tell you."

As she let us into the house, Crystal said, "Take your shoes off, please." I took off my running shoes and looked around. I swear, it was like something out of *The Glass Menagerie*. Every tabletop was cluttered with glass and china objects, although I didn't see a glass unicorn like Laura Wingfield's in *Menagerie*. The walls were covered with paintings, photographs, and posters, all jumbled together. And the carpeting throughout as much of the downstairs as I could see was white. No wonder you had to take your shoes off in the Glass house.

Crystal disappeared down the hall, saying, "Mona, take Abbey upstairs while I check the mail."

Grabbing a corner of my sweatshirt, Mona pulled me up the stairs. "This place is something else!" I whispered. "I've never seen so many . . . things!"

"Wait till you see Crystal's room," Mona whispered back. She pushed open a door. "Crystal calls this her 'cell.' " There was a mattress on the floor covered with a black-and-brown-striped cover, a chest of drawers, and a straight-backed chair in front of a vanity table. A tan, black, and orange rag rug covered the floor.

Crystal strode into the room and began giving orders. "Mona, bring that chair over here. Abbey, sit down and tie this around your neck." She handed me a towel.

Mona stretched out on the mattress as Crystal pulled a plastic cap over my head and tied it tight under my chin. She mixed up the bleach mixture, then began pulling strands of my hair out through the holes in the streaking cap.

"Oh, *really*," she sighed the third time I yelled. "It can't hurt that much, Abbey."

"Want to bet?" I asked through clenched teeth. Then I noticed Mona Lisa. She had tucked her lips in and looked as if she was struggling not to laugh. I hollered again as Crystal yanked a hunk of hair out through a hole in the cap.

"Will you relax?" she asked, exasperated. "You are so dramatic!"

"Well, I'm a little nervous about this. What if you make me too blond, or . . ."

"Honestly, do you really think Mona or I would do anything to make you look worse?"

"You might," I answered promptly, and Mona Lisa burst out laughing. Crystal snapped my head back around.

Then she began heartlessly pulling every hair out of my head—that's what it felt like anyhow. "You're going to thank me when this is all over," Crystal said. I shrieked. "Oh, all right . . . here." She thrust a mirror into my hands. "Maybe that will keep you quiet."

I took one look at myself and gasped in horror. With the cap on my head, I looked like something you might come across in a hospital for the criminally insane. My head is on the small side to begin with, but with the cap on, it looked like a *pea* on top of my neck.

Lifting her face out of the pillow, Mona Lisa made peculiar little sobbing sounds. As long as I had everyone's undivided attention, I took the opportunity to make my infamous rat face. This consisted of baring my teeth and squinching up my nose and eyes. With a scream, Mona collapsed into the pillow again.

An hour and a half later *I* almost collapsed. They had refused to let me look in a mirror while Mona washed and styled my hair and made up my face. When she finally took

me by the shoulders and turned me around to face the mirror—

"Holy Toledo!"

"Do you think everyone from Upstate New York talks like
that?" Crystal asked.

"Jesus, Mary, and *Joseph*!"

"No," Mona said, "just some of them probably. What'd we
promise, Ab? Stunning, hunh?"

I turned my head from left to right, unable to close my
mouth or stop staring at my image in the mirror. My blah
hair had been transformed into a shining puff around my
face, and my eyes were so clear they were startling. I looked
years older. "I . . . I hardly *recognize* myself!"

"You look like a little doll!" Mona said happily. "Now,
remember what I told you about mascara. You put powder
on your lashes *before* mascara."

Said Crystal, "Yes, it makes them thicker."

I swallowed. "Yes . . . and spikier too."

"That's gratitude for you," Crystal said indignantly.
"Look what we've done for her, and she doesn't like it!"

"I'm sorry," I said, quickly. "It's just . . . it's such a
change."

"Wasn't that the whole idea?" Crystal demanded.

Mona offered to give me a ride home, but I turned her
down, saying I was going to run. What I really wanted to do
was sneak into the house and get upstairs to wash my face
before anyone saw me like this. Even to my own eyes I
looked flashy—not like a sixteen-year-old at all.

So I jogged most of the way home and then sneaked
through the woods that bordered our driveway. If anyone
was looking out a window they wouldn't see me. I tiptoed
out of the woods at the back of the house and crept up to the
door. Peering through the window on the back door, I spied
Sheldon slouched over the kitchen table, reading a book. He

was also stuffing potato chips into his mouth and doing something I'd never seen him do before—plucking nervously at his eyelashes.

I knew that he tuned the world out when he read, so I turned the doorknob slowly. Maybe I could still sneak in. I e-a-s-e-d the door open, and . . . Shel looked up. "*Whoa!*" he said, or something like that. It was hard to tell through the potato chips.

"Don't say a word!" I whispered, pointing my finger at my forehead like a gun. "I want to get upstairs before Mom sees . . ."

At that moment she walked into the kitchen, followed by Joyce. Their jaws dropped. Joyce was the first one to collect herself. "Oh, Abbey . . . you look *pretty.*"

"I do? Do you really think so? You don't think it's a little overdone, too much eye makeup? Mom?"

She finally closed her mouth. Then she said, "I really . . . hate it! You look like a grown woman! Please, go wash your face."

But I was already on my way out of the room. Shel called after me, "Leave it, will ya? For once in your life you look decent, man!"

Just as I reached the hall, the doorbell rang and I was up the stairs like a shot. I was crying by that time. I mean, I thought I looked cheap, too, but your own mother could lie a little, couldn't she?

I had just turned on the taps in the bathroom when Joyce came bursting through the door. "Hold it!" She grabbed the washcloth out of my hands. "That boy's here, Ab! The one you like."

"What do you think you're . . . *Joyce!*" I hissed as she began pulling me down the hall.

She stopped and peered up at me. "Wait a second." She went back into the bathroom, ripped a tail of toilet paper off the roll, and came back to me. "Here. You better wipe the

black stuff off from under your eyes. It makes you look"—
she squinted up at me—"like a real tired . . . raccoon."

Outside the living room she pushed a stack of library
books at me. "Pretend you have to put these away in the
bookcase," she whispered. "Now, go on, get in there." She
pushed me into the room.

And there, sitting next to Shel, was Don Champion, looking magnificent in his maroon and white lacrosse jersey and
shorts. Don's green eyes widened slightly as he got halfway
up off the couch. "Is that . . . Abigail?" he asked in an
oddly soft voice.

"You know Don Champion, don't you, Abbey?" Mom
asked.

"We've met," I managed. Then I remembered I had an
armful of books. Don didn't take his eyes off me as I stumbled around the couch and shoved the books any which way
into the first shelf I came to.

"You were saying, Don . . . ?" Mom prompted.

"Oh, yes." He cleared his throat. "Well, you see, Mrs.
Reilly, Coach says we can really use Shel on the team."
Don's eyes followed me as I crossed over to the fireplace.
"And it would be a good thing to put on his college applica-
tions."

"I understand that, but . . ." Mom turned to Shel. "How
can you possibly do everything?"

"Aw, Ma, come on." He jiggled his knee a mile a minute.
"I've *got* to, you know I do. Dad played football *and* lacrosse
in high school. Why can't I play one sport?"

Well, you could see right there and then she was beaten. I
looked at her closely. There were dark circles under her
eyes. Suddenly I wished Shel wasn't so determined. Why did
he always push so hard for what he wanted? Mom looked
completely worn out. "All right," she said. "I suppose you
can . . ."

He bounded off the couch, crying, "Thanks a million!"

Giving her a hasty kiss, he made tracks for the door. "Don't wait dinner for me. I'm going to a party with Don after the game. We'll grab something to eat somewhere."

Don was looking at me. "Would you like to go with us—to the party, I mean? I've asked Mona Lisa, but she wouldn't mind."

I thought differently, but I hesitated . . . until my twin said, "You might as well come, Ab. What else were you going to do tonight?"

Terrific, I thought. Now Don knows I'm a social reject. Then I remembered something. "Aren't we supposed to go to Gram's for dinner?"

"Oh, you're right," Mom said. "I almost forgot."

I turned back to Don. "Thanks anyway, but I can't go."

As soon as the front door slammed on the two boys, I looked at Mom again. She had closed her eyes and was resting her head against the back of the chair. "Boy," I said, "he hasn't been over to see Gram for the past month." I absolutely hated the sanctimonious tone in my voice, but couldn't help myself. "*Boy*. Every time I visit her, she spends practically the whole time asking me about *him*." I started pacing around the room, really getting into my righteous indignation.

Mom said, "I'll have him drive over there to see her some time next week."

"How can he?" I asked, too loudly. "He'll have practice every day, then he has to work at the ice cream parlor. And he'll also . . ."

Mom opened her eyes. "Abbey," she said, quietly, "I didn't want to embarrass him in front of his friend. I'm sure your grandmother will understand. And you *could* have gone with them."

I slumped down onto the couch. "No, I couldn't have. Don already asked a friend of mine to go. He was just being polite, that's all."

"Well"—she shrugged—"it sounded like a sincere invitation to me. I wish you'd learn to exert yourself a little bit, dear. Come out of your shell."

"I have. I mean, I'm trying. I'm going out for track."

"You are?" She brightened up a little. "When did you decide to do that?"

"Last night. Shel was giving me a hard time about being uncompetitive, so I decided to try it."

"Just to show him?" She smiled. "Is that also why you're made up like that? To prove something to your brother? Do things for yourself, Abbey. Run because *you* want to."

"There's just one problem, Mom. I think I really hate to run. Like right now, my knees are killing me just from running a mile."

"I remember what your father told Shel when he went out for peewee hockey." She laughed softly. "The poor kid was the littlest one on the team and he took a pounding in every game. But wouldn't cry until he got home. Your dad used to tell him, 'Pain doesn't last, glory does.' "

"Pain doesn't last, hunh?" I massaged my aching knees and sighed. "I'll try to keep that in mind." Then I went upstairs to wash my face.

Seven

When I was little, about eight or nine, and going through a particularly gawky stage, I convinced myself that my face would grow into my nose and my hair would suddenly behave when I turned the advanced, magical age of thirteen. I thought that once I became a teenager, my troubles would be over—I would know things about life, move gracefully, say the right things. Boys would swoon over me. I would, in effect, be an adult.

When I was eleven I read *Gone with the Wind* for the first time, and Scarlett O'Hara was my ideal woman. Not that she was a sympathetic heroine. Scarlett was selfish, willful, and frequently downright nasty. But she was also in firm control of her world. That was what I admired about her. That and the fact that men fell in love with her at the drop of a hat. When I was little, I dreamed of being just like Scarlett.

So it came as a shock on Monday morning when the new blond, (slightly) made up Abbey Reilly made her debut at school—it quickly occurred to me that having men (in my case, boys) falling all over themselves because of you is not necessarily all it's cracked up to be. In fact, it got pretty complicated.

The first thing that happened was, Packy Cowburn came up to me between fourth and fifth period. His thin eyebrows nearly disappeared under the shock of hair across his forehead as he asked, "What did you *do?*"

"Mona Lisa and Crystal did it. You don't like it, do you?"

He didn't smile, which was unusual for him. Instead he swallowed so that his Adam's apple bobbed. "It's not that I don't like it, so much as I hope . . . I hope you're not going to get stuck up, now that you're so . . . beautiful, Abbey."

I stopped in the middle of the hall to stare at him just as Jack Noon came up. "Hey, Abbey, mind if I talk to you . . . alone?" Taking my arm, he gave Packy a meaningful glance.

Packy sputtered, "Wait a minute—*I* was talking to her!" But Jack had put his arm around me and was walking me down the hall, asking me if I had heard about his wrestling match the day before. I hadn't, so he told me, all the way to chemistry, where Crystal sat two desks away from me.

As soon as the class was over, she came up to me. "What were you doing with Jack?" she asked. "Are you going out with him now?"

"No, he just . . ."

"Oh, you don't have to explain yourself to me," she said, having asked me to explain myself. "After all, *I* was the one who broke up with *him*. And"—she gave me a sly sideways glance as we left the room—"I have Shel now . . . don't I?"

I should have let it go, but I didn't. "What do you mean, you *have* him? You don't own him, Crystal. He's a human being!"

She stopped in front of the room her next class was in and looked at me. "True," she said, raising one eyebrow, "but that means you don't own him either."

"I never said I did," I huffed, but she had already disappeared into the room.

Whoever invented running as a sport must have been a masochist. That afternoon I went to the first practice of my career and got absolutely no pleasure from it, but a *lot* of pain. I thought sports were supposed to be fun, for crying out loud. As I went into my last lap, Ms. Kehoe yelled, "Keep going, Abbey! Don't let up, you're doing fine!"

"Fine my aunt Fanny," I gasped a few minutes later as I limped into the locker room with Mona. "What I'm doing mainly is *dying*."

She laughed. "Keep moving your arms and legs. It's not so bad if you keep moving for a while."

"That makes no sense," I said, flapping my arms and shaking my legs, "but I think you're right. Meanwhile, my body is begging me to lie down and never get up."

"You'll get used to it, Ab. Just hang in there," she said as I eased myself down onto a bench.

Crystal, looking only slightly less cool than usual, pulled her navy blue sweatshirt over her head and looked at me, sweaty and bedraggled. "Your muscles can't go back to rest right away," she said. "If you keep working at it, you'll get used to the physical pain, as hard as that may be to believe right now. But you know, you did fairly well today. I mean, considering it was your first day out."

I pulled off my running shoes and looked at her. Was she serious or not? I couldn't tell. "Thanks," I said finally.

"Yeah, I was impressed." Mona sat down beside me. Her round cheeks were rosy and her thick hair was so damp, it formed deep waves around her face. She looked a little like Botticelli's Venus. "Why am I the slowest one on the team?" she asked no one in particular. "You realize, Abbey, that you beat my time today?"

Crystal slung a towel over her shoulder and looked down at Mona. "You don't care about winning, that's your problem." Turning to me, she added, "Maybe Abbey does."

"Do you?" Mona asked as Crystal headed for the showers. "Do you care about winning?"

Before I could answer, Crystal called back to her, "Have

you decided to ask Don to the picnic, Mona? Let me know, will you?" She disappeared into the shower room.

"What picnic?" I asked. "Ouch!" I groaned as Mona pulled me to my feet.

"It's a class tradition," she answered. "The junior class holds a picnic the first Sunday of spring vacation every year, regardless of rain or snow, which has been known to happen." She went into an empty shower stall and pulled the curtain. "Crystal thinks I should ask Don to go with me, but I don't know. He's okay, but . . ." She trailed off, leaving me hanging.

When a girl came out of the stall next to Mona's, I took it. Raising my voice over the sound of the water, I asked, "Did you have a good time at that party Saturday night?"

"It was all right," she replied as I stepped under the stinging spray of hot water.

I stayed in the shower so long that Mona called, "Abbey! You'll drown!" I turned off the water, toweled dry, and got dressed as fast as I could.

"I was trying to ease the pain," I said, stepping out of the stall. She laughed. "It's not funny. I can hardly walk. I think my calves are knotting up."

"All you can do is keep running, Ab. Wait a sec. I have to comb my hair."

"So . . . you had a good time with Don on Saturday?" I asked, very casual, as I followed her over to the mirrors.

She gave me a look, and for a second I was afraid she could see right through me. "I'm sure you've noticed that I've got a real case for your brother." Mona glanced around to make sure she wasn't being overheard. "Don's okay . . . but he's just not Shel Reilly. And Crystal's so darned competitive, if she finds out, she'll *really* go after him. I'm hoping she'll get tired of him or he of her so I can have him."

"It kills me the way the sexes talk about each other as if we're pieces of meat," I said as we left the locker room.

"I wish Shel would realize I'm alive at least. Oh, well." She sighed. "Crystal thinks I should ask Don to the class picnic. She says I should buy something really slinky to wear to it."

"You think slinky is what's called for at a picnic?" I asked, trying not to laugh.

"You're going, aren't you, Ab?"

"I guess so. But I'm not buying new clothes for it. I'm broke. In fact, I should be out looking for a job instead of running track."

Holding the gym door open for me, Mona said, "Me too. We should dream up a way of making some money. What could we do that would fit into our already busy schedules?"

I stopped just outside the gym and looked at her. "Why couldn't we go into business together? A service business. There are lots of things we can do if we . . ."

Someone called, "Abbey?" I looked up into Jack Noon's sparkly blue eyes. "I just got out of wrestling practice, and I . . . can I give you a ride home?"

Mona nudged me, saying, "Don't mind me. I'll see you later, Ab." She took off down the hall.

"Hey! Mona!"

"Don't worry about me." She faced us, walking backwards. Her grin was definitely diabolical. "I don't mind if you go home with Noonie," she yelled just as Crystal pushed through the gym doors.

"Hello, Jack."

His eyes flicked over her. "Crystal," he said, taking my arm. "My car's right out front, Abbey. I figured you girls were done. I timed it perfectly, hunh?" As he held the door open for me, I glanced back at Crystal. She was standing where we left her. I waved . . . but she didn't wave back.

Noonie had a jazzy black Trans AM Firebird. He put it in gear and roared out of the parking lot. He drove so fast, I gripped the dashboard most of the way. We made it to my

house in record time. "Holy Toledo," I muttered as he came
to a screeching halt at the foot of the front steps. "Do you
always drive like that?"

Stretching a muscular arm across the seat behind me, he
asked innocently, "Like what?"

"Like a complete maniac!" I answered, and he started
laughing. "I'm not kidding, you just took ten years off my
life!"

"I'm sorry. I didn't mean to scare you. I won't do it again,
I promise."

"Well, it wasn't that bad." I felt sorry for him suddenly.
He was so sensitive. You don't expect very good-looking people to be as eager to please as Noonie seemed. "Thanks for
the ride." I opened the car door and started to get out.

"Wait a minute." He reached over, pulling the door shut
again. It was almost pitch-black by this time. There were
lights on in the house. "Can I talk to you for a minute, or do
you have to go in?"

"No, I can talk." I looked at him. "Are you all right, Jack?"
I asked, noticing the way he was gripping the steering
wheel.

"No." He shook his head. "I'm . . . really not all right.
I'm so messed up over Crystal. I need someone to help me,
and I think maybe you . . ." The next thing I knew he had
lunged across the seat, burying his head in my shoulder! "She
said she loved me, and now she's going out with someone
else." He raised his head and stared at me, his face no more
than an inch from mine. "How can you do that? How can
you love someone one minute and someone else the next?"

You're asking me? In a little tiny voice, I said, "I don't
know."

Tightening his arms around me, he buried his head in my
shoulder again. Muffled sounds told me he was crying. *What
should I do?* What would Scarlett O'Hara have done?

Forget Scarlett O'Hara, I told myself sternly. There is

nothing you can do except put your arms around him and try to comfort him. So I did. It was awful . . . but kind of wonderful too. I felt so bad for him it was hard not to cry along with him. We sat like that for what seemed like a long time.

He let me go only when the headlights from another car swept over us. "I'd better go inside now," I said, softly. He brushed his hands over his eyes and turned away from me. "It'll be all right, really it will. Just . . . give yourself time," I said, whatever *that* meant. I had no idea.

As I reached for the door handle, he put a hand on my arm, saying, "Why couldn't I have met you first? You're a really good person. You will help me, won't you? Say you will . . ."

I heard a car door slam and Shel's voice saying, "Thanks for the ride, man!"

"You've got to go to the class picnic with me." Jack shook my arm slightly. "Please?"

My brother's footsteps were coming closer. I said, "I'd love to go with you," and got out of the car just as Shel came up.

"Hi, Ab. Who's that?" He peered into the car as Jack started the motor.

"Just someone from school. His name is . . ."

"Bye, Ab! I'm in a hurry. Got to get to work by seven." He took the steps two at a time.

Eight

At lunch on Wednesday, Crystal put her tray down on the table and sat down across from Mona and me. "What are you two plotting?" she asked, smiling slightly. "I noticed you the minute I came into the cafeteria. You've been talking nonstop."

"Abbey and I are talking about going into business together," Mona answered.

Crystal tasted the cottage cheese salad on her tray and pushed it away. "Business? What kind of business?"

"We're going to advertise ourselves as needy high school students who will do odd jobs," I said. "Like gardening, maybe housecleaning . . ."

"Serving at parties, cleaning up after them." Mona shrugged. "We figure there are lots of things we can do right in the neighborhood. Right, Ab?" She grinned . . . until she caught Crystal's haughty expression.

"Do you mind telling me," she drawled, "how you're going to advertise this . . . business? Advertising is very expensive, you know."

"We've thought of that," I said. "My mother is having about a hundred fliers printed for us in her company's print shop."

"And Dad says we can have the car all weekend to distribute them."

Crystal finished chewing a mouthful of Jell-O. "It's illegal to put fliers in mailboxes, you know."

Very quietly I said, "We weren't planning to put them in mailboxes. We're going to hand-deliver them to people so we can introduce ourselves."

Mona nodded. "Yeah. Abbey figures the personal touch is important so people can see what nice girls we are, that we aren't burglars or something." She started to giggle but changed her mind. "Well, you *could* say something positive about our idea, Crystal. What do you think of it?"

Shrugging, Crystal picked up her milk carton. After a moment I said, "Apparently she does *not* think it's a good one."

But even before the words were out of my mouth, I was sorry. Crystal's eyes filled with tears. "I'm sorry. I know I'm being . . . I'm so upset about my parents. Daddy still isn't home, and I know something's wrong." Before Mona or I could say a word, she got up and nearly ran out of the cafeteria.

"Terrific," I sighed. "Now I feel guilty. I should've kept my big mouth shut."

"It wasn't your fault," Mona said somberly. "I can understand that she's upset about her father—he's hardly ever around. But I know Crystal pretty well, and I think she's more ticked off that you and I are friends. She's kind of used to being the center of attention. Last night she called me up, and at first I thought she just wanted to talk in general. But when she said, 'Mona, are you and I still friends?' I said, 'Of course we are, don't be stupid.' Then she goes, 'I was just wondering.' You know—in that snotty tone she uses sometimes. 'You seem to be spending so much time with Abbey Reilly lately.' "

"What did you say to that?"

"That she seemed to be spending an awful lot of time with *Shel* Reilly these days. Who do you think goes to visit him at that ice cream place where he works?"

"How do you know?" I asked, surprised.

She went red. "Because I happened to drop in on Monday night." She looked so sheepish that I burst out laughing. "Well, how was I supposed to know my former best friend was going to be there?" Mona asked. "I was baby-sitting for a neighbor that night, and when the kids begged for ice cream, I naturally thought of the place where Shel works."

"Naturally."

"You don't buy it any more than Crystal did, hunh?" She sighed. "Well, I don't think your brother did either. Actually, the whole thing was pretty humiliating. There I am with three little kids and I walk in and spot your brother flirting up a storm with Crystal. There's a line of people waiting for ice cream cones, but Shel's talking and laughing with Crystal. And neither of them looked too thrilled to see me.

"Especially when one of the kids dumped his banana split on the floor and Crystal got it all over her shoes, trying to help Shel clean up the mess." Mona paused. "The owner walked in in the middle of all of this and"—she shuddered slightly—"did he yell at Shel! Told him to ask his friends not to come around while he was working. Anyway, Ab, just ignore Crystal. She's jealous of you." I looked at her, surprised. Was she teasing me?

"Oops," Mona said. "There's the bell. See you later!"

Packy hadn't spoken to me ever since Noonie dragged me away two days before, so I was glad when I sat down in English that afternoon and he turned around and smiled. "Guess I'd better quit putting this off and ask you, Abbey— are you going to that picnic on Sunday?"

"Uh, yes, I am."

"Great, then why don't I give you a ride up there?" he asked just as Jack walked by, smiling a hello.

"I can't, Pack. I . . . I have to do something with my little sister that afternoon and . . ." Why couldn't I just tell him the truth, that I'd already said I'd go with Noonie?

"*Her* again," Packy said, disgusted. "I'm starting to dislike that kid, and I haven't even met her!"

"I could meet you up there," I said, fast.

He brightened up a little. "Okay, I guess that's better than nothing."

Wonderful, I thought as Mr. DePace walked into the room and Packy turned back around, I have now committed myself to going to the picnic with Jack and meeting Packy there. But I couldn't tell Packy I was going with Jack. It would've hurt his feelings and . . . "Yes, Mr. DePace?" I swiveled my head around. Everyone was looking at me.

"Are you all right, Miss Reilly?" he asked. "I've asked you twice if you will accept the nomination for short-story editor. Packy Cowburn nominated you."

"Oh! I guess my mind was wandering."

"I guess so," Mr. DePace said dryly, sending a ripple of laughter throughout the room. "Well? Will you accept the nomination or not?"

"She'd be really great Mr. DePace," Mona Lisa piped up from the back of the room. "Abbey happens to be writing a *novel.*"

Mr. DePace's eyebrows shot up to his receding hairline and I wanted to die. I wanted to disappear. "That's *marvelous,*" Mr. DePace said. "Then there's no question about it— may I have a second, please?" He pointed at someone behind me.

"I'll second that," Jack Noon said.

My ears were absolutely burning.

"Any other nominations?" Mr. DePace asked.

"If it's allowed," a girl spoke up, "I'd like to nominate myself for short-story editor." I turned around and met Crystal's icy gaze.

"Certainly," Mr. DePace said, "though I wouldn't have

thought you'd be interested, Miss Glass. English has never
been your . . . strong suit."

When the last bell rang, I took my time getting my things
together, waiting for the room to clear.

"Mr. DePace?"

He turned around from erasing the board. "Yes, Abbey?"

"Would it be . . . can I take a day or two to think about
working on the magazine? I'm worried that I . . . I can't fit
it into my schedule. It would be a lot of time after school and
I run track, you know."

He looked at me silently for a moment before saying,
"Track season ends very shortly, but sure, take a day or two
to think about it if you want." I smiled my thanks and
started to leave the room when he asked, "You're not worried about running against Crystal, are you?"

I stopped and went back to the desk to tell him about my
family responsibilities and all that. But he looked at me with
such understanding that I dropped my eyes. "Possibly," I
admitted.

"Don't let the fear of failure keep you from trying things."

"But I'm new here and everybody knows her. Why would
anyone vote for me?"

"Simple." He began putting papers into his briefcase.
"They'll vote for you if they think you can do the best job."
He snapped his briefcase shut. "Look at it this way—" he
said as we left the room together, "even if you lose the nomination, at the end of it everyone will know who you are. And
you never know, Abbey—you might just win."

I had to run to make it to practice on time. After we had
stretched out for twenty minutes, Ms. Kehoe told us to run
outdoors.

"Thank God for the change," Crystal said as we left the
building. "It gets so tiresome, running up and down the halls
or around the track all the time."

Mona said, "You exaggerate. How many times have we had to run indoors because of rain this spring?"

"About a dozen," Crystal answered. I laughed as we jogged across the parking lot and headed toward Highland Avenue. Crystal looked at me, saying, "It looks as if you and I are running all sorts of races together these days, Abbey."

I nodded. "It does look that way."

"Good," she said, shortly. "Let's see who can run three miles the fastest." With that she took off, easily passing everyone.

"No way you can keep up with her," Mona puffed. "Let her go, Ab. What do you care?"

But I did care. "See you later," I muttered, and pulled away, concentrating on Crystal's retreating form.

At the end of the second mile I thought, *I can't stand this. I really can't stand it.* The pain in my legs was like fire. But then I remembered 'Pain doesn't last—glory does.' *If you were here, Dad . . . if you were only here . . .* I swallowed hard, wincing.

I no longer felt the sun on my back, no longer noticed the yards and houses along the way. When would thinking about my father stop hurting so much? I bit my lower lip and found myself stretching, putting everything I had into my stride. I didn't care anymore whether or not I caught up to Crystal. I just wanted to keep going.

After a while I could tell from the shadows it was late in the afternoon. Suddenly there was a whistle blast. "Hey, you! Abbey Reilly!" I slowed to a stumbling halt. Practice was over. "Don't overdo, girl," Ms. Kehoe said, putting a hand on my shoulder as we walked toward the gym. "You haven't been at this for very long." She opened the gym door, adding, "I have to tell you, I'm very impressed with you, Abbey."

"Thanks," I gasped, wondering if my heart was going to

burst right out of my chest. "I almost killed myself. I did the best I could."

"I knew it—you're going to be one of my best girls," she said just as we rounded the corner in the locker room. Everyone must have heard what the coach said, though it was only Crystal's face I looked for. But she was nowhere in sight.

I sank down on a bench and began massaging my thigh muscles. "Does it hurt bad?" Mona Lisa asked.

"Yeah," I said. "It hurts so much it almost feels good."

Nine

We had dinner as soon as I walked in the door that night because Shel had to be at work by seven. As Mom passed bowls of stew around the table, she asked, as she did most nights, "Anything interesting happen today, kids?"

Shel spoke up immediately. "As a matter of fact, something rather interesting happened to me today. Dr. Kobielski —that's our headmaster—asked me to write a feature story on cheating for our school newspaper. He wants me to determine how big a problem it is at Fitchett Academy, how widespread it is." His voice deepened with importance. "It's my job to find out how much competition for getting into college has to do with academic cheating. I tell you, Ma"—he put his spoon down, frowning intently—"the possibilities for this story are almost endless. I'm going to design a questionnaire, do some real investigative reporting. Of course I'll have to protect my sources. A good reporter always does— right, Ma?"

She beamed at him, I swear. "That's right, dear. Your assignment sounds very challenging. I'm sure you'll do a fine job."

Joyce gave me a look. Then she crossed her eyes and stuck out her tongue. Shel, of course, never noticed. He was too busy talking.

"If it's really good—and I'm planning that it will be, naturally—Dr. Kobielski says I'll get a front-page byline."

"That's wonderful," said Mom, her face all lit up. Suddenly the golden boy groaned, clutching his right side. "What is it?" Mom half rose from her chair. "Darling!"

"It's nothing," he gasped, his face screwed up in pain. "It's just"—opening one eye, he looked around to observe the effect he was making—"a slight injury owing to the unbelievable block I made in practice this afternoon. The guy was twice my size too."

"Why are you laughing?" I asked. "Mo-om."

"Because," she managed, "he's funny."

Joyce and I looked at each other. Neither of us was so much as smiling. Linking my fingers together daintily, I looked around the table. "Well, something rather out of the ordinary happened to *me.*"

Sheldon grinned. "Something extraordinary happened to *you?* Hey, that's a first!" Then he just about fell off his chair laughing.

I waited for him to get a grip on himself before going on. "I was nominated—your sister was nominated—for short-story editor of the literary magazine at school."

"Were you really?" Mom looked at me as if seeing me for the first time. "I hope you get it, Abbey."

I was about to say that I hadn't absolutely decided to accept the nomination when Sheldon piped up, "But what do you *know* about short stories, Ab? Are you sure you can handle the job?"

I resisted the impulse to give him a swift kick under the table. Instead I smiled, saying, "Sheldon, blow it out your ear."

Joyce started laughing as he gasped, "Did you *hear* that, Ma? Did you hear that language at the dinner table?"

She went on calmly eating her stew. Without looking up she said, "I'm sitting right here, aren't I?" Laughing silently,

I jabbed my finger at Shel . . . until Mom added, "I want you to stop whatever it is you're doing right now. That goes for all of you."

Later that evening I finished memorizing the opening lines of Chaucer's *The Canterbury Tales*, which Mr. DePace had assigned in class that day. Everyone groaned when he made the assignment. But after memorizing

> Whan that Aprille with his shoures sote
> The droghte of Marche hath perced to the rote,
> And bathed every veyne in swich licour
> Of which vertu engendred is the flour,

I thought I understood why he made us do it. Chaucer's language sounded far more beautiful to the ear than the modern English.

> When the sweet showers of April follow March,
> Piercing the dryness to the roots that parch,
> Bathing each vein in such a flow of power
> That a new strength's engendered in the flower—

Suddenly the doorbell pierced the silence, making me jump. Joyce's head popped up from the book she was reading. "I hope that's not one of our friends," she whispered. "Mom will spaz out."

Putting a finger to my lips, I pointed at the door. By the time we had tiptoed out into the hall, Shel was already there, still dressed in his work uniform. He must have just gotten home.

He started toward the landing, but I flapped my hand at him and dropped to my hands and knees. It was a cold night, a good night for pajamas with feet, I thought as I crawled toward the landing.

Raising my head, I peeked through the banister . . . and froze. Mom was talking to a big, heavyset *man*. He had his hand propped against the wall over her shoulder. Boy, but she looked small next to him! I could just hear her saying, ". . . nice of you, Kevin, but it's late and my children are upstairs getting ready for bed." At which point Kevin looked up and spied me, lying with my face pushed between the railings.

"So I see," he said, and pointed at me.

By the time Mom called "Get back to your room, Abernathy!" I was already beating a hasty retreat on my hands and knees.

But as Mom finished locking the front door, Shel, Joyce, and I were standing on the landing again. "Who was that?" I demanded.

"Yeah!" said Shel. Joyce was right behind him, her hands propped up on her little hips.

Mom looked up at us. Shaking her head as she came up the stairs, she sighed. "Oh, I pity the poor man who ever tries to call on me."

"Who was he, Ma?" Shel said.

"Just someone I work with. He was passing by and decided to stop."

Said I, "Passing by at *ten thirty?*"

"That's too late to drop in on people, Ma."

"Exactly what I told him. Now you three get into bed."

I watched silently as Mom tucked Joyce in. When she left the room, I followed. "I don't like that man coming over here in the dead of night, Mom."

"I'm sorry, dear. I'll ask him tomorrow not to do that again."

"Well . . . where's his wife?"

"He's divorced."

"*Divorced?*" I said in such a way she looked amused. "You shouldn't have anything to do with divorced men, Mom! I don't like this guy!"

"He's really very nice, Abbey. Besides, you don't know him . . . yet."

"*Yet?*" I repeated, but she smiled and closed her bedroom door. I stood there shivering slightly as thoughts flew through my mind. *Don't tell me . . . just don't tell me that everything is going to change again. I can't stand it . . . I can't stand it if my mother . . .*

Turning, I tiptoed down the hall to Shel's room. He was hunched over his desk, studying. "Shel!" I hissed. "Stop it. You're pulling all of your eyelashes out!"

"Oh, yeah." He looked at the clump of lashes between his fingers. "Guess I'd better knock it off before I pick myself bald, hunh? What're you doing in here, Ab? It's pretty late."

I shrugged and sat down on his bed. "I just wanted to talk."

"About that guy, right?" he asked. I nodded. We didn't say anything else for a while. We didn't have to—I figured both of us were worrying about the same thing.

I listened to the night noises—branches scraping the side of the house, the creaks and thumps of the old oil burner. Mom had said that on the first of May she was turning the heat off no matter how cold it was. I hated her worrying about things like oil bills.

Finally I let out a sigh. "I guess I should let you get back to studying."

He nodded, but as I got up to leave, he whispered, "Hey, Ab?"

"Umm?"

"Crystal stopped by at the ice cream parlor to see me tonight." He paused, studying me. "How come you didn't mention at dinner that both of you were nominated for that editorship?"

I shrugged. "I didn't want you to know. If I lost, I didn't want you to know it was to your girlfriend."

"Heck, I'm glad to see you out there trying. Remember

what Dad always told us," he said, wistfully. "It's better to
try and fail than not try and fail."

I nodded. "I remember."

"Yeah." He smiled faintly. "He sure was a pushy guy,
wasn't he? I wish he'd stuck around longer, don't you? I wish
I'd known him better, but he was never . . ." He looked at
me, then turned abruptly back to his books and papers. I
went back to my own room.

That night I had the dream again. The dream I'd had several times since Dad died, where he's disguised as an old, old
man, something like Father Time in a white toga and a long,
shaggy beard. He is crouched on the side of an icy cliff,
reaching down to me. But there is nothing I can do. I'm just
a kid, standing at the base of the cliff, and I realize there is
nothing on this earth I can do to help him. I wake up crying,
knowing that all I can do is accept that my father is beyond
me now.

At a quarter to six I gave up trying to go back to sleep. As
I came out of my room, I met Shel in the hall. In a hushed
voice he said, "Gosh, Ab, you look terrible . . . as if you've
seen a ghost."

Ten

I was getting books out of my locker just before homeroom when Packy came up with Brian Vaccaro, a boy in our English class. "I wanted to ask you about something Crystal told me and a bunch of other kids a few minutes ago, Abbey."

"What's that, Brian?"

"She said we shouldn't vote for you for that editorship, because she heard you telling DePace you weren't up for it. We figured, you know, if it's true"—he paused—"we'll vote for her."

"Why didn't you say that in class, Ab?" Packy's tone was reproachful.

"I did talk to Mr. DePace after class, but . . . that makes me mad!" I said, suddenly. "The nerve of her, going around telling people that."

"Hey!" Brian put his hands up, sort of laughing. "I don't want to start anything here. If you say it's not true, I believe you. That's why I asked in the first place."

"Spread the word, will you, Brian?" Packy asked.

"Thanks for telling me," I called after him. "*Boy*, that makes me mad, Crystal going around lobbying like that!"

"She's a tough customer, so"—Packy shrugged—"fight for the job."

"How? What am I supposed to do, run around after her, contradicting whatever she says?"

"Why not?" He smiled so broadly, his pointed ears seemed to grow pointier. "You're not afraid of a little competition, are you, Ab?"

"As a matter of fact," I snapped, "yes!" Packy laughed and put an arm around me. "Don't worry," I said, grudgingly, "I'll fight . . . I guess."

"Good for you. And remember what they say."

I looked at him. "What," I asked, "do they say?"

"All's fair in love and war." Then he dropped his arm from my shoulder and took off down the hall.

Lunchtime came and I was still trying to decide what to do about Crystal when she joined Packy and Mona and me at our table. She asked Mona and me, "How are your big business plans going?"

"Great," Mona said. "We've designed a flier." She opened her notebook and took out a piece of paper.

Packy snatched it out of her hands, reading aloud:

"R & R Service has organized in your neighborhood!

"Mona Lisa Roche, Perry Street, and Abbey Reilly, Silverwood Avenue, have formed an *all new* service company to earn funds toward their College Educations."

Mona interrupted, saying, "That was Abbey's idea, putting that part in. She figured it would convince people we're serious about wanting to work. Make them more willing to hire us."

Packy smiled. "Good thinking, Ab." Then he went on reading:

"Let us clean your house, garage, place of business; general yard work and gardening; *serve* at parties (and clean up afterwards); *organize and run children's birthday parties—* "

"Now, that"—I interrupted this time—"was Mona's idea. I think it's a stroke of genius." We exchanged congratulatory smiles.

Packy finished reading the flier and handed it to Crystal, who stuck out her hand. "It's really good," he said. "I just hope you don't get so much work that you don't have time for a social life." He looked at me. "As it is, you run after school, you'll be having meets most weekends . . ."

I smiled at him. Then I noticed Mona's unhappy expression. "You don't think much of it, do you?" she said softly.

Crystal shrugged. "It's all right. I myself don't have time to work. I'm aiming for the States this year and every available minute goes into training. I've set a goal for myself. I want to be first in women's track in the state."

Mona narrowed her luminous eyes slightly, watching as Crystal opened her milk carton—carefully, so as not to ruin her manicure. "There's another reason you don't work, Crystal."

"Oh?" She looked up, pushing a wave of hair out of her face. "What's that, Mona?"

"You don't need the money. Abbey and I do."

Crystal shot her a dirty look, but suddenly her face lit up in a wide smile as she looked at someone over my shoulder. "Why, Jack Noon, where have you been hiding? Come sit by me." She never took her eyes off him as he walked around the table and took the chair next to her. "How are you and why have you been avoiding all of us?" she purred.

"I haven't been avoiding anyone. Hi, Abbey. What kind of food are you bringing to the picnic? Or should I bring the lunch? I don't want anyone accusing me of being a male supremist." He winked at Packy. But I don't think he noticed. He was too busy staring at me.

"You're going to the picnic with *him?* I thought you were meeting me up there, Abbey."

"I was, I mean I am . . ." I looked from Packy to Jack and back at Packy.

"Wait a minute." Jack leaned across the table toward me. "I asked you to go with me when I gave you a ride home Monday night!"

"Yeah?" Packy said. "Well, she told me yesterday that she'd meet me up at the lake!"

Suddenly they stopped glaring at each other and turned to me. "I did, I mean, I guess . . ."

"Abbey Reilly"—Crystal wagged a finger at me—"what a rotten thing to do, playing off one against the other like this." She clicked her tongue. "What would *Shel* say?"

I swear, I wanted to throttle her. But Jack was asking, "Shel? Who's this Shel? You mean you've got a *third* guy on the line? Oh, man, I'm not sticking around for this!"

Crystal reached out and pulled him back down into his chair. "Shel is just a friend of mine," she said soothingly. "He goes to Fitchett Academy. You know, that private school?"

"He also happens to be my . . ." I began, but Packy cut me off.

"I don't know about anyone else," he said, wadding up the remains of his lunch, "but *I'm* getting out of here!" He threw his lunch into a trash can and stalked out of the cafeteria.

No one said anything. Noonie looked at me sadly. "I thought you were different. I really thought you were. I guess I was wrong." He got up and followed Packy.

I wanted to cry. I wanted to put my head down on the table and cry like a baby. But Crystal spoke up. "Don't worry. I'll go talk to Jack, straighten it out for you."

"I'll bet," Mona muttered as Crystal hurried after Jack. "I'll just bet." Then she turned large, reproachful eyes on me. "Did you really make a date with both of them for the same day?"

"I didn't mean to. It was just, I was trying not to hurt anyone's feelings." Mona kept her eyes on me. "Jack asked me first and then Packy did and I really like Packy. He's asked me to do things a couple of times and I've always turned him down and I just couldn't do it again." I sighed, dropping my eyes. "I managed to hurt everyone's feelings, didn't I?"

"I'm afraid so, Abbey. You've also got another problem besides Packy and Jack."

I raised my eyes to hers. "I . . . do?"

"Yep. Now you've got Crystal to deal with. You watch, she'll use this as an opportunity to get Jack back. She won't be able to *stand* it if he recovers from his broken heart so fast. Didn't you see the expression on her face when he asked you what kind of food you were bringing to the picnic?"

I shook my head. "I wasn't paying any attention to her. What was her expression?"

"Like she'd just had the wind knocked out of her," Mona answered, and started giggling. "That swung her for a loop all right. Anyway, you better decide how much you care about Jack, Ab, because . . ."

"I like him as a friend, for crying out loud! Do I have to be his *girl*friend? Can't I just be a *friend* friend? I mean, I like Packy too. In fact, maybe more, because he doesn't come on so strong." As we left the cafeteria, I sighed, asking, "Does everything have to be so complicated?"

"When it comes to the opposite sex," Mona replied knowingly, "I'm afraid things can get real real complicated, Ab. My advice is, Decide how hard you want to fight Crystal for Noonie. I know her, and I know she's going to make a big play for him now that it looks as if he has a crush on you."

A few minutes later I stopped in the middle of the hall, saying, "Wait a second! We've got another problem."

"What?" Mona asked.

"My brother. He really likes Crystal. What about him?"

Mona's face drooped. "Oh, that poor kid. Why can't boys like Shel fall in love with nice girls like me?" she asked, and I might have smiled if she weren't so obviously upset. "Why do they always fall for girls like Crystal? Strike me dead," she said, suddenly taking off down the hall. "Keep reminding me that I've known her for years. I owe her my friendship."

"Friendship isn't based on how long you've known someone, Mona."

"I know. But the thing is, whenever I've gotten into trouble, Crystal has helped me. It started with Ricky Santini in the seventh grade, Ab. All the girls in my class hated me because Ricky loved me."

This time I couldn't help it—I laughed out loud.

"I know it sounds stupid," she said, almost smiling, "but believe me, it was no joke when these two girls threatened to beat me up one day. Crystal defended me. She put her fists up, I swear to God, just like this." Mona demonstrated. "Those girls backed down fast, Abbey. And Crystal's the one who encouraged me to keep running even though I really hate it.

"I was a little chunky in junior high, you know. Crystal suggested I run to lose weight. So I did. Then she encouraged me to stick with it in high school. She says she's not crazy about all the practice either, but it's good for you to do something you don't like. And she's right about that, because I feel good . . . that I have the discipline to make myself do something that's hard." She looked at me, almost embarrassed. "I have more self-esteem than I used to. And I think it's due to the running."

"I guess that's why she's so good at it," I said, half to myself. "Because she's disciplined. I wonder how long *I* can make myself run, and I've only been at it for one measly week!"

"Well, don't give up. Ms. Kehoe says you're a natural, and it would be a crime not to try to beat Crystal. . . . How disloyal of me!" Mona said. "I mean, with a friend like me, who needs enemies, right?" We burst out laughing just as the bell rang.

Eleven

I saw Packy from a distance three times that afternoon. Each time he was talking and laughing with other kids, and I had suddenly become invisible. I made up my mind that I'd talk to him in English. He sat right in front of me, so there was no way he could ignore me there.

Wrong. He slipped into his seat only seconds before Mr. DePace called for our attention. I was so upset by the time class ended that when the final bell rang, I grabbed Packy's arm. "You've got to talk to me, let me explain about . . ."

"No, I don't," he said, coldly. He turned and walked out of the room. I was so shocked, I just stood there until someone touched my shoulder. I turned to find Crystal looking at me.

"You'd better go after him," she said, "and straighten this out."

Jack came up behind her. "He's a good guy, Abbey, the best. So, listen"—he looked at his feet—"why don't we forget about Sunday?" His eyes met mine for a split second. "You and I are just friends, but Cowburn really . . . well, you know. So why don't we make it another time?"

My face felt as if it was on fire. "Sure," I said, amazed at my casual tone. "No problem, Jack."

Crystal said, "Why don't you wait for me in the hall, hon? I have to tell Abbey something. . . . Go on." She smiled up at him. "I'll be right there." He nodded and did as he was told. Crystal turned back to me. "I hope there are no hard feelings, Abbey. But you see, Jack and I have been close for a long time. We still care about each other and . . . well, he also doesn't want to make Packy angry." She paused, waiting for me to say something, but nothing occurred to me. I busied myself with collecting my books. "If I were you, I'd try to talk to him. Explain that you didn't deliberately two-time him."

I looked her in the eye then. "You always think you're the big expert, don't you?" I asked. Before she could reply, I added, "I have some advice for you. . . . I hear you've been going around telling people I don't want to be an editor."

"But that's what I—!"

"I don't care what you thought," I said firmly. "I'd appreciate it if you'd stop putting words in my mouth. It's dirty pool."

She looked as shocked as if I'd slapped her. "I'm sorry, but I did overhear you talking to Mr. DePace, Abbey, and I believe if you want something, you should go after it. That's all I was doing."

I stopped in the doorway and looked at her for a moment. "The least you could do," I said finally, "is deny it and be so obnoxious that I could hate you." We smiled at one another, and for a second I almost liked her.

But then she said, "I myself seem to have gotten into a little trouble over this damned picnic." She gave me a sidelong glance as we walked down the hall. Noonie stepped out of the stairwell, where he'd been waiting for her. "I've already asked your brother to go with me, and Jack, naturally, expects me to go with . . . hi, sweetheart. See you later, Abbey." She wound her arm through his and the two of them drifted down the hall, his dark head bent to hear what she was saying.

Packy was crossing the driveway, heading toward the parking lot, when I caught up to him. "You've got to let me explain," I said, fast. He quickened his pace, refusing to look at me. "I'm really sorry I loused things up, Packy. Chalk it up to a total lack of experience with boys." He gave me a quick look and stopped beside his old blue Ford. "I didn't deliberately make dates with both of you for Sunday," I hurried on. "I just . . . I didn't handle it very well. Please believe me, Pack."

His expression softened slightly. "Come on, Ab. How could a girl like you have no experience with guys?"

"It's the truth. I'm the shy, retiring type, I guess."

His brown eyes searched my face for a moment. Then he said, "How about picking up a little experience this Saturday night? And if you use that sister of yours as an excuse again, I'm going to . . ."

"Saturday would be great, just great," I said hastily, and it might be a cliché, but I swear, it was as if the sun had come out all over his face.

By the time I got out on the gym floor, warm-up stretches were in full swing. But even Ms. Kehoe's dark look couldn't dim my smile. I threw myself into the exercises with a vengeance, stretching my leg muscles until I thought they'd snap. When Ms. Kehoe ordered us outdoors to run, there were groans, but not from me. Today I felt equal to anything.

Two hours later I was changing out of my sweats in the locker room when Crystal asked, "Have you been getting up early to run before school in the morning? You've really improved."

"No, but it's a good idea," I answered.

Ms. Kehoe came to the door of her office, calling across the room, "Keep it up, Abbey. Better watch out, Crystal—she's catching up!"

I laughed, but Crystal took it to heart. "You're not a serious runner," she said disdainfully. "Anyone who is serious runs every morning, including weekends." Then she slammed her locker door shut and swept past me.

"Don't mind her," Mona said, coming up behind me. "You know how Crystal is."

"I don't mind her," I said. "She just helped me make up my mind about something."

Twelve

I was sitting at my desk, studying, when Shel sauntered into the room. "I need to talk to you, Ab. Joyce . . . you mind?" He gave her a meaningful look and she got up and left. "I wanted to tell you that I've got some interesting information for you. It was something a guy said about you."

"Really? Who said what?"

He lay down on Joyce's bed and grinned across the room at me. "First, let's make a little deal. You tell me what Crystal says about me, I'll tell you what this guy said about you."

"How juvenile," said I, loftily.

"Oh, yeah? Well, how about if I tell you the guy was Don Champion?"

Whipping around in my desk chair, I gave him my full attention. "Don said something about me? *What?*"

"O-oh no. Not until you give me the skinny on what Crystal thinks about me . . . though I know already she's pretty crazy for me." He examined his manicure. "She comes down to see me at work almost every night."

"That's not very wise, is it? Won't your boss get irritated?"

"Heck, no." He waved his hand. "You kidding? I'm a terrific soda jerk."

"Overall, I would tend to agree with that . . . except maybe for the soda part."

He laughed good-naturedly. "You're in a good mood tonight for a change, Ab. How come?"

"I just am. Things seem to be going pretty well these days."

Shel nodded. "Yeah, they're definitely going my way too. I've cooked up a hell of a scheme for that newspaper piece I'm working on. The one about cheating? Don's helping me out." He shook his head as I opened my mouth to ask about it. "I'm not telling you anything until the story hits the front page, and man, is it going to hit it! I'm going to impress the heck out of everyone with this one, Ab." His eyes glowed and I was suddenly envious. He always seemed to distinguish himself. You had to give him credit—Shel was full of drive, big ideas.

"So, Ab, you game or not? You tell me what Crystal says, I'll tell you what Don thinks about you."

"Actually, Crystal has another . . ." I shut my mouth. I couldn't tell him about Jack. Not only would it hurt his feelings, but I wasn't sure it was my business to report on Crystal.

"Go on," Shel said. "What's wrong?" His smile faded. "What does she say about me?"

I took a deep breath, "Well, she says that . . ." I paused. The truth was, Crystal had never really said anything about my twin. "She thinks you're . . . quite attractive and . . . she really likes you." I smiled and got ready to hear about Don.

But Shel got off the bed, saying, "You'll have to do better than that, butt breath. I mean, I already *know* that stuff. Who do you think asked me out for tomorrow night?"

"Crystal asked *you* out?"

"Hey, it's a new world out there, Ab. Girls can ask out guys now, if they want. You might take a lesson from Crystal, you know? You'll have to come up with something a little juicier than that if you want to know about Don." He glanced at his wristwatch. "I'd better hustle if I want to make it to work on time. Later, Ab." He left the room, whistling unconcernedly.

Late that night, right after I heard Shel come home from work, the phone rang. A few moments later there was a soft knock on my door. Mom opened it. "I want to talk to you and Shel." She whispered, so as not to wake Joyce.

Shel and I followed Mom into the living room. "What's up?" he asked a little breathlessly.

She stared into the cold fireplace for a minute. "I'm not asking for your permission," she began, "because this isn't something children should decide. But I wanted to tell you that . . ." She took a deep breath. "Your father has been gone for more than a year now, and . . ."

I winced. "He asked you out, didn't he?" Sheldon turned a blank face to me. "That man . . . that man who came over last night."

Mom narrowed her eyes slightly. "Yes, that's what we have to talk about." She sat down on the couch. "But I can already hear in your voice, Abernathy, what you think of the idea."

Shel made a face as if to say "Don't start anything." "I'm sorry," I said, and turned away.

"Kevin Macartney has asked me to go out to dinner and the theater with him on Saturday night, and I've accepted."

I glanced at Shel. There was a muscle twitching in his jaw, the only sign that he wasn't as calm as he looked. Neither of us said anything.

"I know," Mom went on, "that you two have made plans, so I called your grandmother, and Joyce can go there for the evening." Her eyes widened slightly. "What are you doing out of bed?" I turned around to see Joyce creeping into the room.

"I couldn't sleep."

"Your grandmother is looking forward to seeing you, dear," Mom said. "Don't you think that sounds like fun?"

"I guess," Joyce said, hardly jumping for joy. "That's fine, Mom."

But of course it wasn't fine, and everyone knew it. As soon as Mom said we should get to bed, Shel hurried out of the room ahead of me and Joyce. Halfway up the stairs, her lower lip started working like mad. "Hey," I said softly. I guided her quickly up the rest of the stairs and into our room. "It's not that big a deal," I whispered. "All it is, is one little date." She threw her arms around me and hung on as if the world were coming to an end.

"What about Dad, Abbey? What about . . . How can she forget him?"

I sat down on the bed, making her sit beside me. "She'll never forget him, babycakes, but . . . he's gone. There's nothing we can do about it, Joyce. You have to go on, we all do. Besides . . ." I paused, and she turned her tearstained face up to me.

"Besides what?"

"Dad wouldn't want her to sit around for the rest of her life. He wouldn't want that, Joyce. You'll see, everything's going to be fine. Everything's going to be all right." I squeezed her shoulders, thinking *There, I've said all the right things*.

But Joyce shook free of my arm. "How do you know?" she asked. I looked at her, surprised. "You don't *know*, Abbey. Maybe Dad's jealous."

"I *do* know," I said, and tried to smooth her wispy hair, but she pulled away. *She's changing too*, I thought suddenly. My little sister is going to grow up. She won't automatically take my word for it any longer that things will be all right.

And maybe things will turn out all right, but will they ever be the way they're *supposed* to be? That was the real question.

"I don't want her to go." Joyce's sad voice broke into my thoughts. "And I don't want to go to Gram's by myself Saturday night. Will you go with me, Ab?"

I looked down at her small babyish face for a moment. "Sure, kid. . . . I'll go with you."

Even though it was late, I sneaked downstairs to the kitchen to call Packy. His mother answered the phone. Finally he got on the line. "Hello, Pack?" My voice cracked. "This is Abbey."

"Hi, Ab," he said, joyfully. "How are you?"

"Not too good. Listen"—I wet my lips—"I have a problem. I—"

"You're breaking our date," he said immediately. "I knew it. I knew it wouldn't work out."

I couldn't think of a thing to say.

"That's why you're calling, isn't it, Abbey?"

"Yes, but . . ." My voice got higher and higher as I tried not to cry. "I really need you to listen, to understand, because I promise I'm telling the truth." Then I told him about Joyce's reaction to Mom's date, and no matter how hard I tried not to, I cried through most of it. "So," I said finally, "I hope you believe me. . . . Packy? Are you mad at me?"

He sighed. He hates me, I thought. He hates me. I've hurt his feelings for the last time and he'll never speak to me again.

But then he said, "There's no way I can be mad at you, Ab. You're too good a person."

I was so grateful and relieved that it loosened the floodgates again. "I know!" I wailed, and Packy burst out laughing. "Why did I say that?" I asked over his laughter. "I didn't mean that . . . Boy, that makes me sound stuck-up, doesn't it?"

"Oh, Ab, I don't think you could sound stuck-up if you tried. If you can't make it this Saturday, how about three weeks from now? I have to go out of town with my family the next two weekends, so I'm not free until then."

As I hung up the phone I knew I was lucky to have a friend like Packy. He wasn't handsome and I doubted many girls would ever swoon over him, but what I felt for him at that moment was close to love. Besides, three weeks was a long time, plenty of time to get over my fear of being alone with a boy, even one as sweet as Packy.

I paused in the living room doorway to watch my mother. She stood at the windows, her hands behind her back, staring up at the clear, starry sky. "Mom?" I walked over and stood beside her.

In a faraway voice she asked, "Do you know what Joyce told me not long after your father died?"

"No, what?"

"She told me it was all right—I shouldn't worry about Rob. He was safe and living on Mars." She smiled, then turned away, but not before I saw the tears in her eyes.

Thirteen

Saturday morning Shel gave me a ride up to Mona's house on his way to a lacrosse game. We hadn't spoken about Mom's date that night. I guess there wasn't much to say about it.

As if reading my thoughts, he looked over at me. "Strange, isn't it? Having her go out with other men."

I nodded. "Yes, it's—Shel! You're pulling at your eyelashes again. Stop it!"

"Okay, okay," he said impatiently. "I'm just going a little nuts, is all, trying to *do* everything."

"I'm worried about you." I leaned across the seat to get a better look at him. "You *are* plucking your eyes bald!"

"Knock it off," he said, playfully but meaning it. "I can handle it. Don't worry about the kid, man. Hey, I just found out that my school hands out a Most Improved Student award at the end of the year. Guess who's going after it?"

Shaking my head, I said, "No wonder you're pulling out your eyelashes."

"Man, I'm dropping you at the corner." He pulled over. "What I don't need is *two* mothers!"

By two thirty Mona and I had shaken all the hands and done all the smiling we could stand for one day. We had distributed fliers to most of the houses between hers and mine, and had gotten a cleaning job on Saturdays. Another woman hired us to take care of her horse when she went on vacation the same week we had off from school. Some of my friends at home had had horses and I'd mucked more stalls than I cared to mention. I knew I could handle the job.

Mona pulled into someone's driveway to turn the car around toward my house, but I said, "Don't bother. I'll get out here."

"But, Abbey, it's a good two miles back to your house."

"I know, but I didn't run this morning. I need the practice."

"Don't tell me." She slumped in her seat. "You've turned into a running fanatic too. One of the things I liked about you was, you hadn't gone overboard about a sport. Huh!" She sniffed. "Some sport. It's more like torture. Don't tell me you're getting serious about it just like Crystal."

"Not just like Crystal," I said. "But you know something weird?"

"Yeah." She nodded knowingly. "You like running. That's weird all right."

"No, I really don't like it at all. That's why I like it."

She gave me a long look. "Ab, you must be overtired. That makes no sense whatso—"

I burst out laughing. "I'm talking about what you told me last week, Mona. Running has given me some kind of respect, self-respect. You understand?"

After a moment she sighed, looking away. "I know. Oh, Lord." She groaned. "I'm losing you too. I'll be totally friendless," she said as I got out of the car. "I'll finish out my high school career standing on the sidelines, watching as my former friends rush by, covering me in their dust while I . . ." She was still talking as I started down the road.

Thirty minutes later I burst through the front door, looking forward to a long hot bath to ease my aching muscles. Instead I was met by the sounds of the radio blasting over the roar of the vacuum cleaner in the living room. In fact, Mom didn't hear me yelling hello until I unplugged the vacuum and turned off the radio. I had to smile at the way she looked in a pair of my old jeans and sneakers with holes in the toes. "You look cute," I said. "Like a teenager, Mom."

"Thanks—I think. How did your morning go?" she asked. "Is your business off to a good start?" I opened my mouth to tell her, but she frowned, looking around the room. "You know, this room is awfully shabby, but"—she shrugged—"I'm afraid this is as good as it's going to get until I get promoted." She walked over to inspect the double windows. "How would you like to help me wash these, Abbey?"

"Mo-om, I'm beat! I'm absolutely *dead*, I'm . . ."

Chin in hand, she looked the windows up and down. "Thanks, dear. I knew I could depend on you. I'll get the Windex." Before I could say another word, she'd left the room. That's when I realized she was nervous about her date with Mr. Macartney.

I thought you only freaked out over dates when you were my age. I thought by the time you were a *mother*, for crying out loud, you could handle that sort of thing calmly. For the first time, it occurred to me that maybe my mother wasn't much different from me. It was not a comforting thought.

I paced around the living room, thinking, *I cannot handle this. I absolutely cannot handle my mother as a single woman! She has no right to be anything but my mother.*

This made me feel so guilty that when she came back, equipped with paper towels and Windex, I didn't say a word. I began scrubbing windows.

But even as I worked, I got more upset. What about Dad? I kept asking myself. Knowing that I sounded like my ten-year-old sister didn't make me feel any better.

Mom and Joyce and I were in the side yard raking up last year's leaves when Shel breezed down the driveway around five. He climbed slowly out of the car, sort of cradling his left arm against his body.

Mom dropped her rake, calling, "What happened?"

"I broke my collarbone. Coach says I'm out for the season." His face twisted as if he was about to cry. He turned and went up the steps. Mom hurried after him.

Joyce and I looked at each other. "Poor Shel," I said. "Looks as if his lacrosse career was short-lived."

After helping Joyce put the wheelbarrow and rakes away in the garage, I went inside to pack a few things in an overnight bag to take to Gram's. But I was too nervous to get down to it. What if this Kevin person turned out to be a bad actor? What if he was interested in Mom for her *body?*

I stopped in the middle of the room, my eyes wide with horror at the mere thought. Then I began pacing again.

Tears sprang to my eyes. *If Dad were here, none of this would be happening.*

Finally I decided I had two choices—crawl into bed and pull the covers up over my head, or talk to Sheldon.

A minute later, I knocked on his closed door. But there was no answer. "Shel!" I called. Nothing. *"Shel-don!"* Still nothing. I opened the door.

He was out like a light. "Wake up!" I said. "I need you . . . to talk to, I mean." He was lying on his back with his mouth wide open. I made a mental note to mention this to Mona Lisa the next time she got going on how gorgeous he was.

I walked over and prodded him. But all he did was shift position slightly and begin snoring. If I hung around much longer Mom would catch me and accuse me of starting trouble. Suddenly inspiration struck. Leaning down, I put my mouth to his ear. In a normal tone I said, "It's ten of eight on Monday morning and the bus is early."

"Wha—?" He sat up so fast a person with slower reflexes would've gotten creamed by his hard head. "The *bus?"* He

leapt out of bed, wearing only the bottoms to the black satin pajamas Gram gave him for Christmas. His shoulder was taped up. "O-oh!" he groaned, sinking back down onto the bed. By the time he realized what time and day it really was, I was slinking guiltily down the hall. I had forgotten about his broken collarbone. Making him jump out of bed couldn't have been too good for it. But my spirits *were* partly restored.

Five minutes later I strode purposefully into the kitchen. I had decided it was time for my mother and me to have a heart to heart. "Mom . . . ?" She had her head stuck in the oven. "It's not *that* bad!" I yelled. "What're you doing?"

Pulling her head out of the oven, she sat back on her heels. "I am trying to clean the oven. What is the matter with you today, Abbey? You're driving me crazy."

"I know." I sighed, sitting down in a chair. "I'm driving myself crazy too. It's just . . . I'm worried about you, about this man you're going out with tonight, Mom."

Very patiently she said, "I've known Kevin since I started this job, and I promise you he's a very nice person."

"But what do *I* know about him?" I crossed my arms over my chest. "I mean, what do I really know about him, Mom? Nothing! He could be an incipient sex maniac for all you or I know!"

"Abbey . . ." She started laughing weakly.

"Well, I mean you're my *mother*, for crying out loud! There won't even be anyone here to protect you tonight if something goes wrong!"

"I don't need protection. I'm a big girl, and besides that—"

"Besides nothing," I interrupted. "What if he brings you home and wants to come in and— Where are you going, anyway?"

She got to her feet, tucking her hair behind her ears. "Talk about things coming full circle." She shook her head. "This is too much. We're going to the community theater in Westport and . . ."

"What are you seeing?"

"Pirandello's *Six Characters in Search of an Author.*"

"I've read that!" I yelled, bounding out of the chair. "And that's a very risqué play! There's a prostitute in it and . . . !"

Shel, still blinking sleepily, walked into the kitchen. "What," he asked, "is she carrying on about now? Jeesh, you try to get a little rest in this house and this nut's screaming and . . ."

Mom propped one hand up on her hip. "She is giving me pretty much the same routine you gave me first thing this morning."

Said I, "Oh . . . Shel's been over the same ground, hunh?"

Mom turned away, starting to laugh again as Shel said, "Look, Ab, I'm coming home early tonight because of my injury and all. I plan to drop Crystal off around eleven so I'll be here when this guy brings her"—he jerked his thumb at our mother—"home. So don't worry. I've got everything under control."

"Would you two mind," Mom asked, getting down on her knees again, "if I get back to my oven?"

By ten o'clock Joyce was falling asleep over her cards, and Gram and I convinced her to go to bed. Once we'd gotten her settled, Gram slipped her arm around me, saying, "Let's put on warm coats and hats and take a walk on the beach."

We let ourselves out of the house and walked quickly down the path. "I love it out here at night," she said. "And you're the only one of my grandchildren who loves it as much as I." I glanced at her in the moonlight, wondering how she knew. To me, the beach was magical at night, completely different from what it was in daylight. Sometimes I thought my grandmother knew me better than Mom did.

Arm in arm, we walked in silence for a while. There was a

sharp wind, and I was glad for the wool hat and parka I was wearing. Then Gram said, "Tell me, is your mother really coping with everything as well as she seems to be?"

"I think so. I guess I've been so worried about myself I haven't spent too much time wondering how Mom's doing. But I think she's okay."

"She certainly seems to be. You children seem to be in good shape too, though I don't see much of your brother. He's so popular, isn't he?"

"I guess," I said grudgingly, and Gram burst out laughing.

"You and Shel are so funny." She hugged me. "You've always had such a fierce rivalry."

"Yeah, and it's a royal pain in the neck too!" I blurted out. "I hate having to compete against him. He's so good at everything."

"You do pretty well for yourself, my pet," Gram said, reminding me briefly of Dad, who called me that. "Some people claim," she went on, "that children shouldn't be raised to be competitive. They forget, I think, that you don't have to compete to be *the* best, but to be *your* best. That's the key, darling. Use competition to push yourself ahead."

Fog rolled in off the ocean as we walked further down the beach, turning the moon to misty silver. Flecks of phosphorescent material twinkled in the waves as they swept across the sand. I glanced over my shoulder, half expecting to see my father's ghost following us down the beach.

In spite of the wind in my ears, I heard Gram beginning to breathe hard. "Let's sit down on the wall for a while, you want to?" I asked, turning to her. Why, she's *old*, I thought. For the first time, she looked old to me. I realized her salt-and-pepper hair was all salt now. When had that happened?

A sudden premonition sent shivers up my back, but I pushed it away as I sat down on the beach wall. "What do you think Dad would think about Mom going out tonight?"

She gave a little laugh. "Are you asking me if I think he'd be jealous, Abbey?"

"I guess that's it."

"I've wondered about the same thing," she admitted, sighing. "When your mother called to ask me if Joyce could come tonight, my initial reaction was, *But it's so soon.* Then I stopped to think, and it isn't soon. It's been over a year and . . . life is for the living." She spoke so softly, sounded so melancholy, I thought I couldn't stand it. "I think your father, if he knows what's going on with your mother and you children—and I like to think he does—I think he realizes he and your mother were happy for so many years that he has no claims on her now. He wouldn't begrudge her happiness without him, Abbey. I'll always be grateful to your mother . . . for making my son happy for so long."

I ducked my head, wanting her to stop talking about Dad, but at the same time, I needed her to go on.

"You have to learn to let go of people, darling. It's the hardest thing. . . . I learned it when your parents were married. Oh, I was angry at them"—she half laughed, hitting her knee with her fist—"when they announced they were buying that weekly in Upstate New York instead of staying with our family paper. Rob gave up a brilliant career just to have his own newspaper."

"Why did he?" I asked. "I've never really known."

"It's the old story, I suppose, of a child wanting to be his own man. But the real reason . . ." She stopped and glanced at me. "I've always suspected it was partly my fault. When I spoke of competition before, Abbey . . . there's a bad side to it. It can spill over into areas of your life where it isn't appropriate. In the early years of your parents' marriage, I think . . ." She hesitated, staring out over the dark water. "I *know* I competed with your mother."

"I've always sensed some kind of undercurrent between

you two," I said, "but I never really knew what it was
about."

"Your mother has been very kind to me, very considerate,
but I'm sure she resented my efforts to keep Rob near me."
Shaking her head, she went on, "But that is what is so hard
about life—"

I stared at her through the moonlit mist, waiting for the
solution to the mystery.

"Dealing with the constant change," Gram murmured.
"Forcing yourself to do things you're afraid of doing, giving
up things you can't live without. Oh, you know it makes me
so mad sometimes." Her voice changed as she pushed herself
off the wall and stood up. As we started slowly back toward
the house, she kept a hand on my shoulder. "I get so irritated
that I'm at the end of everything. Not because being young
is so much better . . . but you still have everything ahead of
you," she said. "And I've had such a good time," she added
wistfully.

"But that's what scares me, Gram. All of the unknowns
ahead—I'm scared I can't cope, that I'm not up to all of it."

I could hear the smile in her voice as she said, "You'll do
fine. I don't worry about you for a minute."

A steady wind pushed us up the beach and I pulled the
too-big parka more tightly around me. The fog was swirling
around us now, making it hard to see Gram's face. "Do you
really think life is hard?" I asked.

"Yes, I do. You have to work at it. You have to work hard
to make life the way you want it to be . . . or at least a way
you can accept it. It took me years before I could say 'Ah,
now I'm content, now I have all of the things I've always
wanted.' And what happened?"

"I don't know."

"Your father, my only child, got married and moved to the
wilds of Upstate New York. The things that seem so terribly
important at the time! I thought life would never, ever be the

same without Rob nearby. And of course it wasn't. But it was good again."

"Then my grandfather died, right?"

"Yes, then Bob died." She shook her head as we started up the steps which led to the house. "That was a terrible time. I was quite . . . devastated by that. But then you children started coming along, and you came down here every Christmas, every summer. I'll tell you what I'm struggling with now, darling . . ."

"Holy Toledo! You don't mean you're still struggling at your age!" I clapped a hand over my mouth. "I'm sorry, Gram. I didn't mean that the way it . . ."

"But, that's it Abbey!" She turned to me just before we went into the house. "It never ends. The problem now is"— she put both hands on my shoulders and looked me full in the face—"I'm going to be seventy-*five* on my next birthday! I can't believe it! Sometimes I catch a glimpse of myself in a mirror, and do you know it's still a shock sometimes to see this old, wrinkled face?" She laughed, a high, light sound. "I ask myself, how did you get trapped in that old body, a young thing like you?"

Fourteen

The minute we walked into the house on Sunday morning, we heard Mom's tone-deaf voice raised in song. Joyce and I stopped in the kitchen doorway and looked at her. "Hi, girls." Her hands were in soapy water. "How's your grandmother? Did you have a good time?"

"Yes," said Joyce, guardedly. "Did you?"

"I had a marvelous evening." She inspected the plate she had just washed. "Kevin is wonderful company. Abbey, shouldn't you hurry and get ready for your picnic this afternoon?"

"Oh, right. I almost forgot."

Shel sauntered carefully into the room. Holding his left arm against his body, he twirled the car keys with his right hand. "Guess what?" he asked brightly.

I eyed him suspiciously. "What?"

"*I'm* going to your class picnic. Guess who asked me?"

"Crystal Glass. She already told me."

"Oh." He looked disappointed, but only for a second. "Well, guess who's driving us up to Candlegrove Lake?"

"Why should I, Sheldon? You're going to tell me whether I want to hear it or not," I replied. Joyce started giggling.

"Don's driving us. He's going with Mona Lisa Bugg, and he should be here in a half hour or so. You can catch a ride up there with us if you want, Ab."

"No, thank you," I swept past him out of the kitchen. "I am perfectly capable of driving myself."

"Okay." He shrugged. "Oh, and yeah, Crystal asked me to have you call her as soon as you got home."

I swept up the stairs and into my room. Where I slammed the door. Stomping around, I tried to reason with myself. Why was I so upset? I already knew that Crystal had asked my brother to go to the picnic, so what was the big deal? And I had to admit I had gotten to know Mona and Crystal largely because of Shel, hadn't I?

The thing was, I couldn't escape the golden boy. Even when we went to different schools, he took over my friends, my class picnic. I slumped onto the bed, knowing I was being ridiculous. A ridiculous brat, even. For the first time, I realized Gram had done *me* a favor sending Shel to another school. For the first time, I was on my own and I liked it.

Even if he did horn in on *my* friends, *my* class picnic!

One thing I have to say about myself is, I don't hold grudges for long. By the time I had taken a shower, washed my hair, and gotten dressed, I felt better. In fact, when I looked in the mirror I decided I might look like a girl who had taken control of her world. I would show everyone today that Abbey Reilly was strong, that she didn't have to hide in anyone's shadow! Suddenly I felt so good, I tried out some dance steps I saw on a television dance show. Then I hummed a few bars from one of the Top Ten. . . .

The door flew open. "Someone in here with you, or what?" Shel looked around the room, his grin fading. "Man, you are some weirdo. Crystal stopped by to bring you something." He moved out of the way and there she was, ravishing as usual. She wore an expensive tan blazer, designer jeans, and cowboy boots.

"I brought you some clothes I thought might fit you." She came in, closing the door in Sheldon's grinning face. "I haven't been able to wear this outfit for a year because I grew taller, but I think it will be perfect on you." She tossed the dress box onto the bed and opened it.

"Oh, Crystal . . . they're beautiful." I ran my hand over the wheat-colored slacks and angora sweater of the same color. "They look brand-new."

"They just about are. I only wore them a few times. Beige is good on blondes, so naturally I thought of you."

"Thanks a lot." I took the sweater and slacks out of the box and held them up to me.

Crystal looked me over. "You look sweet," she said, "but a little more makeup would help. . . ."

"I borrowed some of my mother's," I said as she put her purse down on the bed and started rifling through it.

"Let me help you." She came over and started putting stuff on my eyes.

"Why are you doing all of this for me?"

As she applied mascara to my lashes, she said, "We're friends, aren't we? Now—" She stood back and looked at me. "Maybe a touch more blusher." She stroked the blusher onto my face, saying, "Sometime, you never know, Abbey, I may ask *you* for a favor. I can help you now, and then maybe you'll help me out sometime, right?"

"Right," I replied uncertainly.

By the time Crystal had finished with me, I barely resembled the all-American Abbey Reilly. A cool, blond stranger stared back at me from the mirror. Joyce came into the room. "Gosh, Ab," she breathed, sinking onto the bed, "I hope I look like you when I'm sixteen."

Crystal smiled. "Well, I'm glad you approve, honey. I myself believe in making the most of everything you've got. Particularly when it comes to boys like"—she leaned over to whisper in my ear—"Don Champion."

I looked at her. "Is that why you've done all this? So I can snake Mona's date?"

She laughed as if I'd made a joke. Giving me a wink, she

said, "Well, I'd better get the car home to my mother. Oh, and one more thing." She lowered her voice. "If Don offers you a ride today, don't take it. And *don't* arrive on the dot of one."

"That," I pointed out, "is two more pieces of advice—and why shouldn't I be on time?"

She sighed, rolling her eyes at Joyce. "Because being on time makes you look too eager."

"Looking eager is uncool, hunh?" I tried not to laugh. She took all of this so seriously.

"*Def*initely," said Crystal in her definite way. "I suggest you leave for the lake at, say, one fifteen."

"But the picnic starts at one and it's a good forty-five-minute drive up there."

"Exactly, my child," she said, and Joyce began laughing. "Sometimes," Crystal said to her, "I think I'm fighting a losing battle with your sister." She turned back to me. "Oh, by the way, did I mention that I—ah—told Jack that I'd already invited someone to go with me today?"

I shook my head and motioned her out of the room. Out in the hall, I asked, "Why did you do that? You knew it would make him mad."

"Well, I had to be *honest*. After all, he and I have been friends for such a long time."

As we started down the stairs, I said, "Oh, great. Now Noonie's jealous and you're using my brother."

At the door she turned to me, tilting her head slightly. "I get it," she said softly. "You're interested in Jack, aren't you, Abbey?"

"That is not . . ."

"Well, you might as well forget it." She opened the front door. "Because I've got him . . . all . . . wrapped . . . up."

"What was that all about?" Shel asked as I stomped up the stairs for the second time that day. "You look mad, Ab."

"I *am* mad! What do you see in her?" I demanded. "She's a snot!"

He burst out laughing. "That may be, but she's an awfully good-looking snot."

By the time Don arrived to pick up Shel, I had calmed down enough to pack my lunch. Unfortunately I was in the middle of slapping together a couple of baloney and Wonder bread sandwiches when the two boys came into the kitchen.

"Hello," Don said in that thrilling low voice of his.

I looked up, prepared to give him a friendly, but not too friendly "Hi." But the instant his green eyes met mine, I fell madly, passionately in love with him all over again. I smiled, speechless, as the blood rushed up my neck into my face.

He crossed the room toward me. He had a slow, hip-swinging walk. It was all I could do to take my eyes off him long enough to stuff my sandwiches into Baggies. There was a sultry expression on his face. . . . I could smell his cologne. He was so close I could feel his warmth. He put his arm around my waist. "How did you get so"—he leaned back slightly to look at me—"*cute* all of a sudden, little girl?"

Now, if I heard that line on television I think I might be tempted to grab my throat and stagger around making loud gagging noises. But it wasn't in the least bit sick-making when this unspeakably handsome boy said it to me.

"How about if I give you a ride up to Candlegrove," he murmured, his eyes fixed on mine. "I can make room for a pretty girl like you."

I swear, it took all of my self-control to look away. "No, thanks. I'm driving myself."

He smiled. "Okay, little girl." Then he planted a whisper-soft kiss on my cheek. His arm dropped from my waist, and he and Shel were gone. I listened to the front door slamming, their footsteps growing faint as they went down the steps.

If I were Scarlett O'Hara, I thought sadly, I would cast my friendship with Mona to the wind.

A short time later I started Mom's car. Suddenly a bright orange sports car roared down our driveway. Out jumped Mr. Macartney. As I drove slowly past him, he smiled and waved as if he'd known me all my life. I considered stopping the car and following him into the house to check him out at close range, but there wasn't time.

Ten minutes later I was bombing up Route 7 in our very uncool tan Chevy. My worries about Mr. Macartney and Mom were behind me. I was so nervous and excited; the butterflies in my stomach were doing a wild tango.

But no one would know. Today the world would see only the new Abbey Reilly, mistress of her fate. I laughed with wild abandon . . . so wild the man waiting for the light to change in the car next to me gave me a really weird look. I also realized I remembered next to nothing about driving from the house to the lake and decided I had better start concentrating on the road before I had an accident.

But no matter how I tried to keep my mind on my driving, the closer I got to Candlegrove Lake, the more excited and optimistic I became. Maybe something terrific and exciting was going to happen today! Maybe Don would realize how charming and witty I was and fall madly in love with me! Maybe he would decide that I was the most fascinating, interesting girl he'd ever met. Once again the world was my oyster—life's possibilities were endless.

I turned the car onto the dirt road that led to the lake. Taking a deep breath, I made a conscious effort to look calm, in control, and decided I could best effect this by sliding down in the seat a bit. This done, I rolled the window down and rested my left arm casually on the car door, steering with my right hand.

It wasn't easy maintaining this ultrarelaxed posture on the bumpy dirt road. But the new Abbey Reilly carried on. I rounded a bend and spotted all the kids gathered on a hill overlooking the lake. It was a magnificent spring day! My heart took wing! Abbey Reilly was on her way to fame, fortune, *romance* . . . Wait a minute. Abbey Reilly nearly got jounced right out of her seat owing to an enormous crater in the road!

I bit back a nervous giggle and waved as Packy stood up, flapping a sweatshirt over his head. "Over here, Ab!" he yelled. Everyone turned to watch as I made my approach.

So I slowed down to about five miles an hour and slipped further down in the seat, leaning heavily on the door. With expert ease, I turned the car into the parking area and . . .

THE CAR DOOR SWUNG OPEN, SPILLING ME OUT ONTO THE DIRT!!!!

There was a roaring in my ears, and my knees were killing me. Dazed, I looked up and . . . HOLY TOLEDO! *The car was still moving!* I jumped up and raced after it, leaping into the driver's seat just in time to save my mother's car from rolling down into Candlegrove Lake.

By the time all the kids reached me, I was draped, exhausted and panting, over the steering wheel. Everybody was yelling and asking questions at once.

"I can't believe what I just *saw!*" Mona Lisa gasped. "That was unbe*lie*vable, Abbey!"

"Man, you take the cake, you really do. If Ma ever saw that, you'd never get the car again!"

"How in hell did you *do* that, Abigail?"

I put my head back down on my arms. "Abbey?" It was Packy. "Are you all right? Better get out now, okay?" He opened the door.

Crystal pushed her way through the crowd. "I believe in making an entrance," she said, "but that one takes the cake. How *did* you manage that?"

"I have no idea," I answered shakily as Packy took my arm. She took my other arm, and they helped me across the field as someone backed Mom's car up. The other kids scurried ahead of us, one or another glancing back at me from time to time.

Stopping suddenly, Mona said, "O-oh, look at her knees." She clapped her hand over her eyes as I looked down at the shredded knees of Crystal's formerly elegant slacks. It must have been a shock reaction or something, because my legs gave out.

I couldn't see for a few seconds. When my vision cleared, Packy's face was close to mine. "You really did a tune on yourself. God, Abbey, you could've even . . . killed yourself."

"Yeah." Don squatted beside him. "That was truly amazing all right. Hey, Shel! Your sister's some piece of work!"

Packy shot Don a look before turning back to me. "I've got a first-aid kit in my car," he said. "I'll go get it."

Don slapped him on the back. "Yeah, Cowpie, you do that!"

"The name's Cow*burn*, buddy."

"Right, guy," Don said, smoothly. "No offense meant." He smiled as Shel came over.

"Man, you're bleeding like a stuck pig. Come on, Don, you grab her legs, I'll get someone to take her arms."

I was just about to tell Sheldon what *he* could do in no uncertain terms when Don said, "I can carry her by myself, Reilly." And without further ado, he scooped me up into his arms.

I swear, it was like something in a novel, Don carrying me over to the blankets spread out under a clump of trees. It was the most romantic thing that had ever happened to me. As Don gently lowered me to the blankets, everyone crowded around, eager to see how bad my injuries were. Some of them were laughing about what an unbelievable crack-up that Abbey Reilly was. I didn't pay much attention, though.

All I could think about was Don . . . until I noticed Packy's face as he walked toward us, the first-aid kit in his hands.

Wordlessly he knelt in front of me and opened the kit. "Well," Don said, standing up, "I guess I had better find my date. Are you going to be all right, little girl?" I nodded, sneaking a look at Packy.

As Don went off in search of Mona, Packy cleaned my knees and bandaged them. "Thanks a lot," I said when he had finished. "What would I do without you?"

Without meeting my eye, he said, "He's the one you really like, isn't he?" I opened my mouth to protest, but he gestured impatiently. "Please . . . don't deny it. I'm not blind, Abbey. It's all over your face." He pushed everything back into the first-aid kit and stood up.

"Pack"—I grabbed his ankle—"don't get mad. . . . You and I are friends!"

"Haven't you figured it out yet? I don't want to be your *buddy*, Abbey. Hasn't that occurred to you?"

"What are you talking about? I thought . . ."

"Look," he said quietly, "it kills me, the way you look at that big guy."

"But I didn't . . ."

"Abbey, it's not that I blame you. I'm no movie-star type. I know that . . ." Right then I understood an expression my mother often used about her heart going out to someone, because at that moment my heart went out to Packy Cowburn. "Let's face it," he said with a sad smile. "I'm funny-looking, and you aren't . . ."

"Packy, you're not!"

He shrugged, turning away. "Never mind, I know when to quit. See you around." He started to walk away, then he stopped and looked back at me. "Are you . . . crying, Ab?"

I bit my lower lip and nodded, unable to look at him.

"I'm sorry. I didn't mean to upset you," he said, coming back and kneeling in front of me. "Wow, you're really *bawl-*

ing," he added, making me half laugh, half sob. He handed me a red bandana from his back pocket and sat beside me.

We didn't speak for a while, just sat there watching a softball game someone had organized. Finally I said, "Nothing ever turns out the way you imagine it will, does it?"

Why did life have to be so complicated? I mean, Don was my masculine ideal—he was so handsome and smooth—but Packy was my ideal too. He was funny and kind, the way he turned to me now, saying, "Sometimes I think things work out the way you hope they will, Ab. You have to hang in, keep trying."

"But, Pack, I never do anything right. I try to act suave—you know, as if I know what I'm doing. Instead, I . . . *humiliate* myself in front of the entire class!"

"Oh, I wouldn't go *that* far. I wouldn't say you humiliated yourself exactly. I mean, you can't help it if you act sort of goofy sometimes."

I looked at him. "I don't think you're making me feel better, Packy." He started laughing. "I don't think you're helping."

"But, Abbey, I'm glad you're a goofy little kid—don't you get it? That's one of the things I like best about you! Who cares what anyone else thinks?"

That's when I noticed Crystal and Mona. They were standing apart from everyone, hanging on to each other. I could see their shoulders shaking. Mona must have felt me looking at her, because she suddenly turned. Our eyes met. She nudged Crystal, making her turn around too. The three of us stared at one another.

Then, very slowly, Crystal swung her head back and forth. The next thing I knew, Packy, Mona, Crystal, and I were laughing. And I was thinking, *This is perfect. This moment right now I want always to remember.*

Then I happened to notice Shel—mainly because he was

standing all by himself, leaning against a tree. The way he cradled his left arm to his body, I knew his collarbone must ache. I caught his eye, and he smiled faintly. There was something in that smile—was it envy?

Fifteen

When the sun began sinking and a rising wind whipped the water in toward shore, the picnic broke up. Packy was helping me to my feet when Don came over. "Hey, little girl, would you like to go to a party over in Stamford? A friend of mine is throwing a little do."

"A *do?*" Packy repeated, but Don ignored him. He draped an arm around me and moved away . . . taking me with him.

"What about Mona Lisa?" I asked.

"Let's get something straight, sweetheart," he said in a confidential tone. "I go out with lots of ladies. No one, but no one, ties me down."

"I didn't mean you were tied down, but Mona asked you to come today. I think I'd better drive myself home." I twisted out from under his arm just as Mona Lisa came up, lugging a wicker basket in one hand and trailing a few blankets in the other.

"Hey, Abbey?" she panted slightly, blowing a curl out of her eyes. "I meant to tell you we've got a garage-cleaning job tomorrow afternoon for a lady who lives down the street from me. I hope you can do it. I promised her R & R Service would be there."

I spotted Packy slowly making his way across the field toward the parking area. Turning back to Mona, I said,

"Great. I'll come over to your house around one, okay?" But I didn't wait for an answer. I ran after Packy.

Just as I reached Crystal and Shel, suddenly my twin stopped. "Who's that?" He pointed at the black car that was skidding up the road, sending up a cloud of dust.

"Oh, my God!" Crystal put a hand to her mouth. "It's *Noonie.*"

"Who's Noonie?" Shel asked as she fell back a step.

The black Firebird squealed to a halt. Noonie leapt out. "Crystal, get over here!"

"Who *is* that?" Shel asked again as Mona hurried up to us.

"An ex of Crystal's," she answered. "Uh, oh, he looks as if he's been drinking." I looked at Noonie as he came toward us. Mona was right. His face was flushed and he was weaving slightly.

"Oh, I was afraid of something like this happening," Crystal moaned. "I—I don't know what to do." She turned fearful eyes on my twin. "Shel?"

"You were afraid, hunh?" Mona said. "Is that why you made sure he'd know you were here with someone else?"

Shel went "*Shh!*" I suddenly realized that while he might be as tall as Noonie he was nowhere near as broad and powerful-looking. Not to mention his broken collarbone.

Don sauntered up, asking, "Hey, who's the hood?" Then he yelled, "Hey, muscle man! Buzz off! She's with us." He slung an arm around Crystal and grinned at Noonie.

Crystal had never looked more gorgeous. Her eyes were wide with excitement, and the wind blew strands of hair across her pale face. She looked like a heroine on the cover of a Gothic novel. "Oh, Donnie!" she cried, hugging him. "Do something! He's got a terrible temper."

"No sweat," said Don. "I can handle that dude." He put Crystal behind him and walked up to meet Noonie. "Now, look here, buddy, Crystal happens to be an old friend of mine, nothing more."

"Are you the one she's with?" Noonie asked. His light-blue eyes were so bloodshot they looked purple.

"I was *afraid* he'd make a scene," Crystal said, latching on to Shel's left arm. He grimaced, but didn't take his eyes off Don and Noonie.

Meanwhile, Don had taken a pack of matches out of his pocket. He lit one, flipping it to the ground at Noonie's feet. "Now," he drawled, "on the count of three, I want you to turn around and go back to your car like a nice guy, okay? One . . . two . . ." Noonie didn't budge. "Three," said Don. Grinning, he lit another match and flipped it. This time it bounced off Noonie's chest.

"Man," Noonie murmured, "you're asking for it."

"Don! Don!" Mona Lisa tugged at his sleeve.

When Don struck the third match, Shel, chuckling nervously, walked up to them. "Listen, friend," he said to Noonie, "I'm with Crystal today, but I'm taking her home now, so if you want to talk to her . . ."

"Once more, buddy," Noonie warned Don. "You do that one more time . . ."

Don held up the lit match and Mona Lisa yanked his arm. "I'm trying to *tell* you," she shouted, "that he's the *captain of our wrestling team!*"

Don's head snapped around as he stared at Mona. When Noonie brought his arm back, Shel stepped forward, and good old Don ducked. The punch caught my twin square on the jaw. "Jack, don't!" Crystal screamed as Shel reeled over backwards.

As Noonie started toward Shel again, I looked around wildly for help. Don was running for the parking area. . . . Packy's car was gone. I looked back at Shel. He was half crouched, shaking his head and trying to clear it.

"Oh, honey, are you hurt bad?" Crystal wailed, hanging over him. Meanwhile, Shel's lower lip was starting to look like a hamburger. Blood trickled from one nostril.

There's no help for it, I thought. It's up to me. Taking a flying leap, I landed on Noonie's broad back. "That's my brother, you bozo!" I yelled, grabbing a handful of hair.

Noonie hollered, "What the—! Reilly, will you . . . ? *Ow!*"

"I'm not letting go until you say you'll quit," I yelled as he stumbled around, trying to shake me off. Years of defending myself against Sheldon paid off. "Are you going to quit?"

"You're something *else!* Ouch!" He shrieked as I gave his hair a good yank. "You're killing me! Okay, okay, I won't hit him again—I promise." I let go and slid off. "Cripes," he muttered, squinting at me as he rubbed his head, "you're some tiger."

Everyone stared at me. Crystal's mouth hung open while Mona Lisa had both hands pressed over hers. I couldn't tell if she was trying to keep herself from laughing or from crying. Shel got wearily to his feet. The five of us stood there silently for a moment.

Finally Shel spoke. "I don't know what this is all about, but if you're all through," he said to Jack, "I'll take Crystal home now. You two can discuss whatever the problem is without me next time, okay?" Putting a hand to his bleeding nose, he walked away.

Crystal started to run after him, but Noonie pushed her aside. "Hey, man!" he called. "Wait up!" Shel stopped and turned around. "I want—I guess I should . . . apologize." Shrugging slightly, Noonie stuck out his hand. "I'm sorry, man." Shel looked at the outstretched hand a little dubiously at first, but he finally shook it.

Then Noonie said, "So, *you're Abbey Reilly's brother,* hunh?"

Shel smiled wanly. "Yeah, as a matter of fact, I am. Are you really the captain of the wrestling team?"

Noonie nodded, smiling kind of sheepishly. "Where do you go to school?" The two boys walked away, leaving Crystal standing alone.

Mona turned to her, saying, "It didn't turn out the way you had in mind, did it?"

"What are you talking about?" Crystal tossed her head and started to follow the boys.

"I think," Mona said mildly, "that you just convinced two nice guys never to have anything to do with you again. That's what I hope, anyway. You can be pretty rotten sometimes. Now I'm going to find big Don and tell him to take me home."

"Wait a minute!" Crystal said, angrily. "What about that party in Stamford?"

"What about it?" Mona asked as she walked away.

"I thought the *four* of us were going. Mona!" Crystal stamped her foot. "You're supposed to be my friend!" Mona kept going. As I passed her, Crystal said, "Abbey?" I kept going too.

By the time I got behind the wheel of the car, it was almost dark. I had just turned the key in the ignition when Shel rapped on the window. I rolled it down. "If you don't mind," he said, "I think I'd better drive us home. Even with a bum shoulder, I think maybe I handle a car better than you, Ab."

I was about to tell him what *he* could do when Crystal opened the passenger door and got in. It was too dark to be sure, but she looked as if she'd been crying. Without a word I got out of the car and climbed into the backseat.

No one said anything on the way to Crystal's house. When Shel pulled up in front and made no move to walk her to the door, I knew how angry he was. My twin was nothing if not a gentleman.

After sitting there for a moment, Crystal sighed and got out of the car. She leaned down, saying through the half-open window, "Good night, Shel . . . and thank you," in the tentative voice of a little kid who has just thrown a tantrum and is trying to make up.

He barely glanced at her. " 'Night."

As I climbed out of the backseat, Crystal said, "Maybe we could run together this week?" She sounded so eager, I felt sorry for her. But only for a moment, because when I hesitated, she added, "Don't feel you have to do me any favors. I've run alone for years. I guess I can make it through one more week."

I paused, one hand on the car door, and looked at her. "Could you help me with my start?" I asked finally. "Ms. Kehoe says my timing is off."

"I'd be glad to. I'll call you in the morning."

"Okay," I said, and got into the car.

Shel started the engine as Crystal waved and went up her porch steps. "That was nice of you, Abbey."

We exchanged a brief look. I nodded. The thing was, I thought as he backed down the driveway, it wasn't my fight. It wasn't my job to pay her back. We could fight with each other, Sheldon and I, we could help each other cope with life. But I couldn't make things turn out right for him any more than he could for me.

Sixteen

We didn't speak until we were almost home. Shel said, "Would you do me one favor?"

"It depends on what it is."

"Well, I appreciate the way you came to my defense, Abbey, I really do. But I don't think what you did was too smart. You never know, the next time you jump on some guy's back, he might haul off and let you have it."

"That's gratitude for you," I grumped. "I didn't have a whole lot of time to think about what I was doing, you know. I just . . . acted."

"I know, and I have to say . . . I really admire you for it."

I peered at him, trying to see if he was putting me on or not. "Are you feeling all right? Are you sure that punch to the head didn't affect you?"

He laughed a little. "What's the story with Crystal and that guy, anyway?"

"They had a hot and heavy affair, and she spurned him for—"

"Ab, I don't think it's funny."

"I'm sorry." After a moment I turned to him again. "Don't tell me you really like her, Shel, because . . ."

"It's not just her." He sighed. "It bothers me, sure it does, that that Noon character showed up. . . ."

"Crystal made *sure* he'd show up!"

"He *is* in your class, isn't he?"

"But she . . . !" I began.

"Look, Abbey. I'm not stupid. I know Crystal's type—a little too good-looking for her own good, and she knows it."

"Then why do you bother with her?" I asked after a moment.

"I guess because she's a challenge and we all know I can't resist a challenge. The thing is, I'm striking out on all fronts these days, Ab. I'm a lousy athlete, a failure with women . . ."

"That's not so! Why don't you give Mona a chance, Shel? She really likes you."

"She does?"

"Sure she does, and you don't pay any attention to her." Even in the dark I could tell that made him feel better. "Mona may not be as 'challenging' as Crystal, but she's a really nice girl."

"I know she is, but I can't do that to my buddy, Don."

I sniffed, remembering the rear view I'd gotten of Don as he made tracks for the safety of his car that afternoon.

Shel turned the car into our driveway. "Hey, you know, I just remembered something I've been meaning to tell you— Bassett Hunter asked me about you the other day."

Keeping my tone ultracasual, I said, "Oh, really?"

Shel started laughing and pushed my shoulder. "Way to go, hunh, Ab? Man, you're just knocking guys dead these days . . . when you aren't leaping onto their backs, that is."

For the split second before the house came into view, I felt wonderful. The world was my oyster. Then I spotted the bright orange sports car parked at the foot of the steps. "*He's* still here!"

Shel turned off the ignition. "So? What about it?"

"Doesn't that guy have a home of his *own?*"

"Listen, this gives us the perfect opportunity to sneak upstairs without having Ma see us and start asking a lot of questions. Besides, Abbey, she's entitled."

"To what?" I snapped as we went up the front steps side by side.

"To her own life. So . . . grow up."

"I'm trying to. Has anyone ever told you," I hissed as we let ourselves into the house, "that you can be a very irritating know-it-all? Not to mention that your nose is starting to resemble a squashed tomato." I clapped a hand over my mouth.

"Oh, yeah? Well, you look as if you fell out of a moving car!" He ruffled my hair and went bombing up the stairs, chortling like a crazy person.

At nine o'clock Mr. Macartney was still downstairs in our living room. We kids were on vacation the next day, but Mom had to get up and go to work. Joyce and I were in the window seat, reading. She was, anyway. I was stewing over how to get rid of Mr. Macartney.

Shel looked into the room. "Hi. What're you doing?"

Both Joyce and I were sitting there with books in our laps. She rolled her eyes and sighed. "Why," she asked, "does he *always* do that?"

"Do what?" I asked.

"Ask questions he already knows the answer to," she replied, which prompted Sheldon to come over and start tickling her. Naturally Joyce started laughing and carrying on.

I flapped a hand at them. "Keep it down, you bozos!"

"Yeah, Joyce," said Shel, "quit making such a racket when Ma's entertaining a gentleman caller." His grin faded. We listened to the faint but steady drone of voices from downstairs. "You'd think they would've run out of things to talk about by now, wouldn't you? Don't you think it's time that guy went home, Ab?"

I nodded. "Maybe Mom needs help getting rid of him," I

said, and Joyce nodded eagerly. "Maybe she doesn't know how to do it politely!"

"Yeah!" said Shel. "Let's see, what can we do to help her out?"

"I'm the best eavesdropper in the family." I climbed over Joyce out of the window seat. "I'll sneak down there and find out what's going on so we can decide how badly she needs us."

"Good idea, Ab. Joyce and I will wait here."

I tiptoed down the stairs and across the hall to the utility closet, which also housed our stereo. A pair of cabinet doors opened directly into the living room. It was a perfect setup. By putting an ear to the crack in the doors, I could hear almost as well as if I was in the room with them.

"I suppose," Mr. Macartney was saying, "I'd better get moving."

Slight pause. Then Mom said, "Yes, it is getting late."

I knew it! She wants him to go!

Mr. Macartney must have stood up, because his voice wasn't as clear. ". . . had a great time last night, Evelyn. It's been a long time since I've met a woman I can talk to as easily as I can to you."

Mom murmured something but I couldn't make it out. I heard them walking across the room, so I eased myself around, being careful not to knock into the vacuum cleaner or mop. I put my eye to the closet doors and . . . *boy*, but it gave me a weird feeling, seeing him kiss her. And boy, was he kissing her!

I had to bite my lip to keep back a rush of tears. For the first time in my life, I wished I weren't spying. I wished . . . Wait a minute, he was saying something.

". . . consider going into the city for the weekend, Evelyn? I haven't spent a weekend in town in years, and we could see the top hits on Broadway."

Holy Toledo! That big oaf had just propositioned my little

mother! I was about to leap out of the closet to go to her aid
when Mom said, "Why, thank you, Kevin. My children
would love that. They've been after me since we moved here
to take them into New York and . . ."

Mr. Macartney burst out *laughing*. He grabbed Mom's
hands, saying, "Oh, I do like you, Evelyn. I really, really like
you!" and they started laughing together!

He left (*finally*) and Mom locked the front door after him.
She had to turn toward me to turn off the hall light, and in
that instant before everything went dark, I caught a clear
glimpse of her face. . . . She hadn't looked that happy since
before my father died.

As she went upstairs, I heard Shel call out to her to come
into his room. It gave me time to get back to my own before
she looked in to say good night to Joyce and me.

Moments after Mom had closed her bedroom door, Shel
put his head into the room. "What went on down there?" he
whispered. Joyce popped up from under the covers, all ears.

"Not much," I lied. "Go to bed. I'll tell you about it tomorrow." But as he made a move to leave, I added, "We don't
have to worry about Mom, though. She can take care of herself."

Seventeen

"Can you believe," Mona stage-whispered, "anyone saving *112* coffee cans? It's bizarre!" She looked around Mrs. Winch's garage, her round face clearly expressing dismay. "I mean, we've been in here ten minutes and we haven't even started cleaning it out yet."

"What do you mean *we?*" I said. "I've made a dent in the work table. You're the one who's poking around looking at things instead of cleaning up. Besides, it's probably not that many cans. It just looks like a lot."

"Ab, I counted them. There are 112!"

I tossed her a plastic garbage bag. "Well, start bagging them and get them out of here. That's what we've been hired to do."

Mona muttered, "When Mrs. Winch offered me this job, I figured no sweat, clean out a little old garage. I had no *idea* . . ."

I didn't hear the rest. I was too busy hammering nails into the wall to hang garden tools on. That done, I loaded the rapidly filling garbage bags onto a wheelbarrow and trundled them out of the garage.

Two hours later Mrs. Winch stood in front of her neat and tidy garage, shaking her head. "How did you do it? I can't believe I'll actually be able to park the car in here."

Mona Lisa pointed at the huge mound of junk to be carted

away by the garbage men. "You should probably check to see if we're throwing out anything you might want to . . ."

"Don't say it!" Mrs. Winch put a finger to her lips, glancing at the house. "I want all of this *out* of here before Mr. Winch decides what he can't live without. Like his coffee cans. I've never seen him use a one." She smiled. "And now if he does get angry about whatever has been thrown away" —she looked at Mona and me—"why, I can blame it on you girls!" She paid us the agreed-upon rate, and we left.

We had almost reached Mona's house when she said, "You know something? I've been thinking that cleaning up that garage was worth more than we charged. Maybe we should charge by the job for certain things."

"You mean give people estimates according to the job?" I asked. She nodded. "Maybe you're right. We can try it. Actually, we're already doing that. Mrs. Grabinski's horse, remember?"

"That's right. We start with tonight's feeding, in fact."

"I'll do it. I'd rather you do the morning feeding because it's closer to your house. We'll trade off mucking the stall every other day, okay?"

"Fine," Mona said. "We certainly work well together, Ab. Do you think we're going to get rich?" She laughed. "One thing I'm not doing this vacation is running."

"Well, I'm going to keep at it. Crystal and I ran this morning. She says I have to run further every day if I want to increase my aerobic capacity."

Mona rolled her eyes. "Speaking of Crystal, how's your brother? Did he say anything about what happened?"

I shook my head. "I haven't had much time to think about all that. Don called this morning, though, and there was something odd about it. . . . Shel made plans to go up to school this afternoon." I frowned.

"What's odd about that? Maybe they have a lacrosse game or something."

"No, that can't be it. Shel's off the team, and his school is closed for spring break too. What was unusual was"—I glanced at her—"Shel was whispering into the phone."

"Where were you? Hovering right outside the door?"

"Of course," I answered. "Listen, I might be a world-famous novelist someday. Eavesdropping is a good source of material—look at it that way."

"Well, I don't think it's odd that Shel was whispering, especially when he knows what a nosy type you . . ."

"There was something else, though, Mona. He mentioned French windows a couple of times."

"French windows?" she repeated. "I've heard of French doors, but never windows. Maybe he meant doors. Oh, well. . . . Do me one favor? Find out if Shel is still going out with Crystal, but don't say I asked or anything."

"All right. The only thing I know for sure is he thinks she's a challenge."

Her face fell. "And no doubt he loves a challenge, right?"

"Afraid so. I think that may be one of Shel's greatest strengths."

"Or weaknesses, Ab. It depends on how you look at it."

Eighteen

Spring break went fast. In addition to taking care of Mrs. Grabinski's horse every day, Mona and I got a window-washing job, and Mrs. Winch called again. This time to clean out her cellar. It took us three hours and we charged a flat rate, which meant we each made a little more per hour than what we had been charging. We were beginning to act like businesswomen.

I also ran early every morning with Crystal. We met at a halfway point on Silverwood Avenue and ran for at least an hour. There was something companionable about being the only two people on the street so early in the day, often before the sun had burned off the ground fog. I began to appreciate her silent, determined company. The only time she spoke was when she coached me. "You've got to practice your start over and over, Abbey. It's the only way you'll excel."

I kept expecting her to bring up what had happened at Candlegrove Lake, but she never said a word. Until we were back in school on Monday.

Mona and I had just walked into the cafeteria when Crystal came up to me. "I've got to talk to you. Could you come sit with me in the courtyard?" She turned to Mona, saying, "It's private. You understand, don't you?"

"What's the problem?" I asked as soon as we sat down.

Her words came out in a rush. "I am so miserable. I've been waiting for Shel to call, but he hasn't. Maybe you could talk to him?" When I didn't say anything right away, she added, "I've helped *you* all week. The least you could do is help me when I need it!"

"Why don't you call him and apologize for . . ."

"Apologize?" Her eyes widened as she twisted around to face me. "Why should I apologize for what Jack did?"

"Okay, don't apologize." I stood up. "Why did you ask for my advice if you're not going to listen to it? You're the only one who can help yourself. I can't do any—!"

"You're right," she said hastily. "I'll call Shel tonight. If you really think it will help." She looked up at me.

"It can't hurt. And I think he might like to hear from you." I grinned.

She smiled, saying, "You know, I'm really starting to like you." She sounded so puzzled, I burst out laughing.

Our newfound friendship, or whatever it was, lasted only until the end of practice that afternoon. As all of us crowded into the locker room, Ms. Kehoe called out, "Abbey Reilly, you're ready to represent us in the fifteen hundred meters against Darien on Saturday. Keep up the good work!"

"Nice going," Mona said as I sank onto a bench beside her. "Ms. Kehoe must think you're pretty hot stuff." She jabbed an elbow into my side. "That's Crystal's event, you know. Won't she just *freak* if you beat her?"

Behind us, a voice said, "Won't Abbey just freak when I become short-story editor tomorrow?" I turned around just as Crystal slammed her locker door shut. Then she turned and strode out of the room.

Mona clapped a hand to her forehead and groaned. "Oh, boy. I just put my foot in it again. I'll see you at the car, okay? I'd better go talk to her, try to calm her down."

The phone rang during dinner that night. Usually Mom didn't allow phone calls during the dinner hour, but she let me take this one because it was for R & R Service. When I came back to the table, Shel said, "Did you get another job?"

"I'm not sure. I'm going to have to discuss it with Mona. . . . I'm not sure it's something we want to tackle."

"What is it?" Mom asked.

"Mrs. Tamburo—the lady across the street—needs someone to scrape that toolshed at the edge of her property," I answered. "I told her I'd talk to my partner about it and get back to her." I picked up my fork and began to eat.

After a moment Shel said, "I'll do it."

I looked up. "What about your collarbone and when would you have the time?"

"Heck, I'll *make* the time, and it hardly bothers me. You and Mona can take a percentage of whatever I make. That's fair, isn't it? I need the job, man."

"Well, I'll talk to Mona about it."

"Gosh," said Joyce. "My sister the businesswoman."

I blushed, thinking, *What do you know—I've become a pacesetter, no longer a shadow sitter.* That's when I noticed the hint of envy in Shel's face again. "Did your girlfriend ever call?" I asked. "She said she was going to." I grinned, thinking that would pep him up.

But all he said was, "Yeah. . . . She called."

"I think," said Mom, "your brother is more concerned about losing his job today."

"You lost your *job?*" I repeated.

Shel nodded, lowering his eyes. "My boss says his profits started dropping practically from the day I started work. He says I was overloading the cones . . ."

"Overloading the *cones?*"

"What are you," Shel snapped, "a parrot? He also said he wasn't crazy about all the girls who congregated in the shop the nights I worked." He moved the food around on his plate, avoiding my eye.

"Oh, well," I said after a moment, "I guess that's the price you pay for being so charming, right?"

"Really," he said, heavily.

"Well, don't worry. You can work for R & R now." I shut my mouth, realizing how that must sound.

But he said, "Thanks. At this point, I need all the help I can get."

A half hour later I was sitting at my desk, trying to study. Mom and Joyce had gone out to do the weekly grocery shopping and I could hear the rapid fire of Shel's typewriter coming from behind his closed door at the end of the hall. He'd been working on the feature story for his school newspaper for the past week, even during vacation. The success of the story was probably even more important to him now that he'd been fired.

The golden boy certainly was having his problems, I thought . . . and wondered why that didn't give me at least a little bit of satisfaction. Hadn't I been striving to beat him, to be better at something? Wasn't that what going out for track was about, and the main reason I had decided to try for the editorship?

A sudden thought brought my head up out of my history book—*what if Shel gave up?* It sent me scuttling down the hall to his room. I was just about to knock on his door when the front doorbell rang.

"Hi," I said, surprised to see who was on the front doorstep. "Shel's upstairs, but I'll go . . ."

"I didn't come to see him," Crystal said softly. "May I come in?"

"Sure." I opened the door wide. "What's on your mind?" I asked, walking ahead of her through the hall.

"I have a proposition to make," she said. I stopped in the

middle of the hall and turned to face her. "Don't look so suspicious!" She laughed. "It's something that will benefit both of us."

In the living room she curled up in a corner of the couch the same way she had the first night I met her. I sat down in the wing chair and waited. "Let's be upfront with each other," she began. "You really, *really* want to be short-story editor, while it isn't all that important to me, correct?"

I shrugged. "If you say so."

"You also know that I have to qualify for the States this spring."

"Why do you *have* to, Crystal? What will happen if you don't make it? Will the world come to an end?"

"You don't understand. I've set a goal for myself. And I'm *going* to do it." She spoke with such determination I had to admire her.

More kindly I said, "I know how important running is to you . . . but what does it have to do with me?"

"I have to win all my events on Saturday, Abbey. I absolutely have to!"

"Well, you're the best girl on the team, so I'm sure you . . ."

"Nothing is a sure thing!" Her voice was loud in the silent house. "I've been thinking about withdrawing my nomination tomorrow. You know, I only nominated myself so you wouldn't run unopposed. I mean, how *boring* that would be, right?" She laughed again. "I really didn't think it through very well. And now I've decided that . . ." She poked at the hole in the worn corduroy fabric. "I've decided that it just isn't very important to me, but"—she raised her eyes to mine and, I swear, hers gave off sparks of light—"it is to you, Abbey."

"What are you proposing?"

"I'll go to DePace before class tomorrow afternoon and tell him I want to withdraw. And you . . . if you run extremely well on Saturday"—she dropped her eyes and began fiddling nervously with the sofa cushion—"you . . ."

I finished it for her. "Let you win."

"Exactly!" She smiled, relieved. "I mean, we're friends, after all, and friends help each other out, right?"

"No."

"*No?*"

"No. I mean, yes, friends should help each other, but no, I won't let you win on Saturday."

"You won't!" She was completely shocked. "You mean, you *won't* do it?"

"Yes . . . I mean . . ." I stuttered as her face darkened. "No, I won't set up our event for you. You'll win because you're the best. What would it mean if I let you cheat?"

"I only proposed this as insurance," she said angrily. "You're new in school, let's face it. I know everyone! I have a much better chance of winning tomorrow. You're stupid not to take advantage of . . ."

"Maybe," I said, and her mouth drew into a thin, straight line. "But maybe not. I'd rather take my chances."

Not long after Crystal had marched out of the house, Mom and Joyce got home. "Who was that?" Mom asked breathlessly as she took off her raincoat. "She nearly ran into us at the end of the driveway."

The phone rang, saving me from having to answer. "May I speak to Mrs. Reilly?" a man asked.

"Yes, you may," I answered. Then—I couldn't resist it—in my best honeyed tone I asked, "Is this Mr. Macartney?" Mom's head went up and she came over and tried to get the receiver away from me.

"No," the man on the other end said patiently. "This is Dr. Kobielski, headmaster of Fitchett Academy."

"Oh!" I said, shoving the phone into my mother's hands. Joyce and I hovered in the kitchen doorway, listening. But we couldn't get the gist of it because Mom wasn't *saying* anything. But then she started saying, "Oh, no. Oh . . . *no.* I can't believe he'd do such a thing!"

That's when we knew Sheldon was in trouble.

Nineteen

All day in school the next day, I wondered what Shel's punishment was going to be. He had broken into his school during spring break to steal a French exam. It had something to do with his newspaper piece about cheating.

I watched Mr. DePace counting paper ballots. At this very moment, I thought, Mom is talking to Dr. Kobielski. Maybe they'll expel him. Maybe they'll . . .

Mr. DePace finished counting the ballots. The minute he looked at me, I knew I had lost to Crystal Glass.

Mona and Packy came up to me at the end of class. "Sorry about that," Packy said. "I guess you can't win them all, and all that rot."

Mona nodded. "I want you to know I didn't vote, Abbey. I abstained because I couldn't choose one of you over the other."

"That's okay," I said. "I understand. Congratulations, Crystal," I called out as she passed us. "I'd like to be on your committee if that's okay."

"You know something, Abbey?" She shook her hair out of her face.

"What?"

"You give me a . . . pain in the *neck*. You're such a sanctimonious *simp!*"

Amazed, I said, "But all I said was . . ."

Crystal was red in the face. "You make me ill the way you go around acting so holy all the time. Isn't anything important enough to you to make you fight? What *is* important to you, besides maintaining your Goody Two-shoes image?"

Then she tossed her amber mane and walked out of the room. "The nerve!" I finally managed, turning back to Packy and Mona.

"I think," said Mona, "I'd better get going. I have to see someone before practice." She beat a hasty retreat.

I looked at Packy, asking, "*Am* I a simp?"

He smiled. "I don't think so, Ab, but what's more important is . . . what do you think? Are you going to let her get away with calling you one?"

The minute I got home that night, I headed upstairs to Shel's room. "All right," I said, barging in without knocking, "what did the headmaster decide in the big meeting today?"

He was lying on his bed, staring at the ceiling. "They've decided not to suspend me . . . because they believe my intentions were honorable."

There was silence. Then I said, "I swear, your luck is incredible."

"Really, Ab. I have such incredible luck, I convince myself I can pull *off* a dopey stunt like that." He turned his head to look at me. "Don talked me into it. He said, 'You'll make a hell of a mark around here if you can pull this off, Reilly.' And like a jerk I fell for it!"

"I'm starting to dislike that guy," I said, angrily. "Is he taking any of the blame for this?"

Shel shook his head. "Why should he? All he did was suggest the idea."

"*And* provide the key to the French teacher's desk," I pointed out, somewhat acidly.

"Well," Shel said morosely, "I'm not turning him in. If he can't face the music himself, I'm not going to tattle on him."

We were quiet for a few seconds, and then Shel said, "Just because I wanted to be a star, make a big impression. I actually thought they'd reward me for showing how easy it is to cheat! I planned to submit the exam with my copy, you know, thinking the teacher would have enough time to write a new test so there'd be no real harm done." He looked at me. "How do I talk myself into believing that breaking and entering is ever justified, Abbey? Do you *realize* how much trouble I could've gotten into? Just because I wanted to be the best."

"But I've always admired your drive."

"Well, don't. Look where it's gotten me." He struggled into a sitting position and ran his hands through his hair. "I've been doing a lot of thinking since I got home from school . . . and I've decided something. I'm going to try to be more like you, Ab."

"Sheldon, I've been trying to be more like—!"

"I saw you at that picnic. People like you, Abbey. I can tell."

"Yeah? Well, they don't like me all *that* much. I lost the election for the lit magazine this afternoon." I sniffed indignantly. "And the only reason I finally made friends was because you practically forced me to! Besides, you've got friends. . . . You've got . . . Crystal, for one."

He shot me a dark look. "Oh, really. Did you know she has a date with that Noon character this Friday?" He nodded at my surprised look. "I called her yesterday, like a dope, and I got the distinct impression that she *loved* telling me she was busy."

I could feel the blood rush to my face. "Fine," I said, shortly. "You've just given me another good reason to beat her on Saturday. And I'm going to . . . if it's the last thing I do."

Shel smiled. "Way to go, Abbey, but just remember one thing . . ."

"What's that?"

"It's only a sport. Winning is not the most important thing in life. I just figured that one out." He flopped back down on his bed.

I paused at the doorway and looked back at him. "You might be right. But maybe the most important thing is trying to win, *I* just figured *that* out."

Twenty

Saturday dawned rainy and cool. I woke up at five, unable to sleep because of the butterflies in my stomach. I started worrying about the track meet and closed my eyes again, trying to calm down.

An image of the gym flitted across my mind: everyone lined up, waiting for the gun. . . . I saw myself . . . saw myself get a perfect start, pull ahead, winning . . . *I saw myself win the race.*

Once, long ago on a rainy day like this, I overheard Dad lecturing Shel about the technique of preparing yourself to do something difficult by mentally envisioning your own success. I had been skulking around the house, eavesdropping, when I heard Dad in the library. He was lecturing Shel. . . .

Wait a minute. . . . I opened my eyes. Dad *always* lectured Shel. I tried to remember the two of them just talking about something and couldn't. It suddenly seemed so one-sided—Dad's voice, virtual silence from Shel. No wonder he was so driven!

Long before my event began, my stomach was so queasy I was scared I'd be sick in front of everyone. The bleachers were filled. I tried to pick out Mom and Joyce, but I couldn't concentrate.

When the starting gun finally went off, I got a bad start. In spite of all that practice, I was caught off guard. But I fixed my eye on Crystal's back and gritted my teeth. *I am going to win.*

Natural runner, natural runner; Ms. Kehoe's words pounded through my brain, keeping pace with the stinging slap of my feet against the gym floor.

By the third lap I had left most of the others behind and was gaining on Crystal. Not that I was racing against her any longer. I had gone down deep inside, barely aware of the hollow roaring in my ears, the people, bits of color, on the sidelines. The most important thing was to keep running as fast as I could, to endure the pain.

I am going to die. This is so hard I am going to die.

Finally she and I were side by side. She'd pull ahead, I'd catch up. I'd pull away, she'd match me. I glanced at her once—there was real agony in her face. "My record!" she gasped. "My winning streak!"

I looked away, and the corners of my mouth twitched up into an awful, involuntary smile—*I was going to beat her.*

But in the next moment I felt a painful jab in my side. Her hand darted out again . . . I stumbled . . . whistles blew. Anger, like color, exploded in my brain as a runner from the other team crossed the line ahead of us.

People rushed up to me as the nausea I had fought all morning overcame me. I doubled over. "It's all right," someone said. "Take it easy."

Mona Lisa was there, yelling, "Somebody get her something! Gatorade!"

They pulled me over to a bench. "Leave her alone." Ms. Kehoe's voice came from far away. "Put your head down, Abbey." I felt a hand at the back of my neck. "You'll be all right in a minute. It's not uncommon." She went on talking calmly as I struggled not to vomit again. I was dry-heaving so hard there were tears in my eyes. Gradually the sickness began to pass. Ms. Kehoe was saying, "Sometimes you get a runner who wants to win so badly she literally makes herself sick."

I looked up at the faces of my teammates. That was me Ms. Kehoe was talking about—a runner who wanted to win that much.

Mona Lisa elbowed her way through the circle of girls. "You came in third, Abbey." She waited until Ms. Kehoe got up and walked over to speak to the other coach. "You should have been first."

"We saw her," someone said. "We saw what she did."

"Did the judges see?" I asked. They shook their heads.

"I don't think Ms. Kehoe caught it either," Mona said, "or she would've given Crystal holy you know what. But never mind . . . we'll take care of her."

"What are you going to do?" I asked.

"We can lodge a formal protest," someone said.

Another girl spoke up. "Keep her out of the States."

"No"—I got to my feet—"I don't want you to do that. It's not that important." Everyone started talking at once. "Look," I said, speaking above their voices, "I was the one she hit. I'll take care of it. And you're forgetting something —Crystal also lost."

Mona looked around at everyone. "It *was* Abbey's race." She turned back to me, asking, "What are you going to do?"

"Nothing," I said. "I'm not going to do a thing."

Twenty-one

"Why didn't you tell us before now that he's going to be here in half an hour?" Shel asked, angrily. "I need more notice, Ma!"

Mom looked surprised. "I asked Kevin to come here for dinner rather than take me out again. Restaurants are expensive and . . . I don't see what difference it makes to you, Shel."

He stood in the middle of the kitchen, an indignant expression on his face. Then he turned to me, saying, "Help me!"

"With what? I've already made the salad and Joyce did the bread."

Joyce's eye met mine briefly. "All she's serving is spaghetti," she told Shel.

"That's not what I meant, and you know it. Okay, I've made plans to go out tonight, but don't worry about it." He started toward the phone. "I can change them. I was only going over to Bassett's for a while. He won't mind if I . . ." He began dialing.

"Honey," Mom said, taking the phone out of his hands and hanging it up, "Mr. Macartney is coming over to have dinner with me." She put the slightest emphasis on the last word. "I want you to go out and see your friends. Now, I'm going upstairs to take a bubble bath."

"A *bubble* bath!" Shel shot me a look. "Since when do you take bubble baths?" he called after her as she left the room.

The three of us looked at each other. Then Joyce said, "All he's doing is coming over for dinner. He took me and Mom out to lunch today, you know, after your track meet, Ab."

Sheldon sniffed and began stalking around the kitchen again.

"He told me I could order whatever I wanted," Joyce went on. "Do you know, I've been thinking about it . . . and I don't think I ever went out to lunch with Dad. To a real restaurant, I mean."

Shel stopped circling the table. "Dad had a deadline to meet every week, Joyce. How was he supposed to take you out to lunch when he worked every day? Besides, you were just a little kid. You weren't old enough to go to a real restaurant. Besides, who wants to waste a perfectly good Saturday or Sunday going out to *lunch?*"

I was about to tell him to calm down when Joyce spoke up. "I'm not complaining! I'm just saying I never went out to lunch with my own father. It's true!" She turned to me, her eyes welling with tears. "Is that wrong? To say that?"

"No," I said. Shel turned his back to us. He put his head in his hands, leaning against the sink.

"Everything is so different," he said softly. "It's just that . . . everything is so different."

"I had *fun* going out today," Joyce said. "We went to that fancy place by the waterfall. I was the only kid in the place! I liked it!" Her voice rose. "And I liked Mr. Macartney!" She got up and ran out of the room.

Shel looked at me. "I guess I came on too strong."

"She'll get over it," I said, watching him. "Why are you so upset all of a sudden? Just a week ago you were telling me to grow up about Mom and her . . . friend. So why are you so upset about it now?"

"I don't know. I guess because I'm scared . . . she's going

to—everything's going to— We've got to stick together on this one, Ab. Help each other get through this."

I nodded. "When haven't we?"

"True." He stared at his feet for a moment. Gradually the pucker between his brows smoothed out, and he looked at me again. "You know something, Ab? Sometimes I almost like you. Sometimes you're not so bad."

I was about to thank him when he had to yell, "Even if you are a little *butt breath!*"

By the time I was up out of the chair, Sheldon was racing up the stairs, carrying on like a wild man.

On Monday Ms. Kehoe started me on a new training program. She told me to sprint for a specific distance, over and over, for half an hour every day. She said it would increase my aerobic capacity, which would in turn improve my speed. And she gave me the same advice Crystal had—run further every day. I groaned inwardly at the idea, but didn't dare show anything but enthusiasm to Ms. Kehoe. She had such faith in me, I couldn't let her down.

By the time I got into the locker room that afternoon, it was deserted. But when I stopped at the water fountain for a drink I heard voices way down in the last section, where my locker was.

Crystal's cool voice reached me. "Meet you at the car?"

There was silence. I finished drinking and straightened up, wiping my mouth.

"Mona?" Crystal's voice was louder. "I asked you a question."

Finally I heard Mona's high-pitched voice. "You know, Jennifer, I've been thinking about buying leg weights. If Abbey Reilly"—she raised her voice as she said my name—"and I keep raking in the dough from our business, I'll be able to afford them in no time."

Jennifer asked, "You're really doing that well, you and *Abbey Reilly?*"

"Oh, the business is booming. It was all Abbey's idea, too, you know. She's the brains behind R & R Service."

Then Crystal said sharply, "I get it! You're giving me the silent treatment, aren't you?"

"She's not as stupid as she looks," someone said. "Maybe when she apologizes for what she did, we'll . . ."

"Oh, no," another girl said, "not until she also tells Kehoe she shoved Abbey."

I stepped around the corner—and nearly got run over by Crystal as she tore past me, running down the length of the room. The gym door whooshed shut after her. I turned back to my teammates. "Hi there, sport fans."

Mona giggled, and you could feel the tension ease. "Hurry up and change, Abbey. My mom needs her car tonight."

About a mile from school we spotted Crystal walking quickly along the side of the road. Mona pushed the gas pedal down and sped by her. "Come on," I said. "Stop and give her a ride. It's not out of your way."

She shook her head. "Nope. I'm not having anything to do with her until she admits to what she did. I think making one of your own teammates lose really stinks."

I sighed. "What if she refuses to apologize?"

"Then she can remain friendless and despised," Mona replied, and she was dead serious. "If being number one is so important to her, fine, she can be it. If winning is that important to her . . ." She shrugged. "She's made her choice, hasn't she?"

By the end of that week I almost felt sorry for Crystal. Every time I saw her, she was alone. Even Jack Noon seemed to be giving her the cold shoulder. I spotted her once or twice trailing in his wake in the halls. I might have spoken to her, said hello at least, except she never gave me the chance.

By the time I got into the locker room every afternoon, Crystal was already out on the track. She made sure she was the first one off too.

As for my twin—I told Shel what had happened at the meet and all he'd said was, "Really?" and shook his head. The thing was, both of us had other things to worry about. Shel spent every afternoon that week trying to find another part-time job. Mona and I subcontracted with him to scrape Mrs. Tamburo's shed on Saturday morning, but he needed more than one odd job. And when he wasn't job hunting, he was either studying in his room or playing mournful tunes on his guitar.

I was used to *me* falling into the pit of despair and having Shel there to jolly (or bully) me out of it. But when *he* got down, I didn't know how to help except to leave him alone.

I could also see that Mom was driving him as crazy as she was me. Mr. Macartney called her every night, which was fine. What bugged me was the way she went around *beaming* after each call. Part of me was glad for her, I think, but another part—the nasty side, I guess—found her happiness almost nauseating. From the dark looks I caught Shel shooting in her direction, I could see that his resentment was growing too.

The other thing that had me on edge was that the first date of my life was rapidly approaching. This coming Saturday was my date with Packy. I was actually going to be alone with a boy. In a car. For a long period of time. Just thinking about it was enough to send fear rippling up and down my back.

So I was caught off guard on Friday afternoon when Mr. DePace asked me to stay after class. He waited until everyone had left the room, then said, "Crystal has withdrawn as short-story editor. She says she has too many other commitments to do an adequate job. Naturally you would be the one to replace her. Are you willing to take it on?"

A month ago I probably would've dithered around, looking for excuses for why I couldn't do it. Now I didn't hesitate. "Sure," I said. It was as easy as that.

Wrong! Mr. DePace whipped open his briefcase and took out a thick stack of paper. "Here are a few stories that have been submitted for consideration. You'll have to organize a committee, read these, make your selections with written recommendations, and get them back to me in two weeks time. Crystal hasn't done a thing."

As I staggered from the room, clutching the stack of stories to my chest, he called after me, "Congratulations! I know you'll do a fine job."

Twenty-two

Five o'clock on Saturday afternoon found me curled up in the fetal position with the bedcovers pulled up over my head, trying to will away a severe stomachache. I kept asking myself, *Why are you scared? You know Packy. You know he is a good, kind person.*

But another part of my mind kept saying, *I'm not scared, I'm not scared . . . I'm terrified.*

The phone rang. I knew it had to be Mona Lisa again. She had called at regular intervals all day to give me tips on how to behave on a date.

Sure enough, a few seconds later Shel yelled up the stairs, "Abbey, it's for you!"

I raised myself up on an elbow. "If it's Mona, tell her I'm *out*."

His feet thundered up the stairs. My door flew open. "It's not Mona, it's someone else. Make it snappy, I gotta make a call."

So I dragged myself out of bed and across the hall to Mom's room. I picked up the receiver and said, "Hello, Mona."

"I'm calling to say I'm sorry," Crystal said, "for the track meet."

"Oh . . . thanks."

"I'm not apologizing because anyone told me to," she

added, with a hint of her old arrogance. "I want you to know I didn't think about what I did. It just . . . happened."

"It's okay. I accept your apology. But, Crystal . . . don't do it again." I lowered my voice. "Because if you do, I'll scream bloody murder. And even if you had won, you wouldn't really have, you know."

There was a pause. Then she asked, "How do you mean? If you come in first, you come in first. You win."

"But the whole team saw you cheat. They knew what you did. In their eyes you were a loser, Crystal. No matter what any judge might have said. Do you understand?"

"Well, that's one way of looking at it . . . I suppose." Her tone changed. "Tell me, how's your handsome brother these days?"

I knew it! He's the reason she apologized. "You ought to know how he is," I replied. "He's going out with you tonight, isn't he?"

"No. . . . I asked . . . just now . . . and he said he already had plans."

"Oh!"

"Did you . . . did you—ah—mention what happened at the meet last Saturday?"

"Yes, I did."

It was her turn to say "Oh!" She got off the phone in a hurry after that. I was halfway down the hall to Shel's room when the phone rang again.

"Hel—"

"Ab, it's *me.*"

"Hi, me."

Mona Lisa went into her high-pitched giggles. "There's just one more thing I have to tell you."

"It can't possibly be something you haven't already covered. You've only called fifty-two times today."

"I want you to have a good time tonight, that's all. Now, Abbey, I want you to fake interest in whatever Packy talks about tonight. Even if it is the most *boring* subject in the world, act interested."

"How does one fake interest, Mona?"

"*You* know."

"Obviously I do not know or you wouldn't keep calling me!"

She dissolved in laughter again, but managed to say, "You smile and nod and everything like that to show him how fascinated, and all, you are by him. Like when Don gets going on what a terrific lacrosse goalie he is? I pretend I haven't heard it fifteen times before. Get it?"

"How come you encourage him? You don't seem to like him much."

"Oh, I'm not seeing Don anymore," she said, brightly.

"You're not! I thought you told me you were going out tonight."

"I am!"

"With whom?"

"Your brother!"

"That's great! But . . . What about Crystal?" I asked.

"What about her?" Mona asked. "She just called me to ask if I minded if she called Don Champion, they had been friends for *such* a long time and she was *so* lonely. I told her, call him, I couldn't care less.

"Now, to get back to your date, Ab, if Packy gets going on something you're not even remotely interested in, you just smile and nod, you know, make little comments, maybe, to show him that you're . . ."

"Mona, I have to tell you something. I can't do any of that nonsense. I'll go along with just so much, but I *refuse* to act stupid just to flatter a boy." There was dead silence at the other end. "I really appreciate everything you've done to help me," I added hurriedly, "but I can't act dumb just to make Packy feel macho. Course I agree it wouldn't be too cool to start *snoring*." She burst out laughing, cutting me off.

As I hung up the phone, Mom yelled up the stairs, "Abbey! Shel! I need some help straightening up before Kevin arrives."

"Coming," I called back. She sounded freaked out again. I rolled my eyes to the ceiling as I started down the stairs, wondering how long this thing with Mr. Macartney was going to last. Shel and I had discussed it and decided that once she got tired of him, life would get back to normal.

"Watch it, will ya!" Shel said, nearly toppling me to my death. "Hey!" He grabbed my arm, stopping me in the middle of the stairs. "Did I ever tell you what Don said about you, butt breath?" He smiled winningly, flipping his hair out of his eyes.

I tried and failed to get away from him. Sighing, I said, "Sheldon, I have already fallen for that line once. You're not doing it to me again."

"He said something wicked nice about you, Ab. He checked you out at that picnic a couple of weeks ago. I promise you this time, you tell me what Mona Lisa Bugg says . . ."

"SHELDON!"

"Roche, I mean Roche. *Jeesh*, you don't have to break a guy's eardrum. Anyway, you tell me what Mona says about me, you know, then I'll tell you what . . ."

I put my hand on his shoulder, looked him straight in the eye, and said, "Forget it. Holding Don Champion over my head won't work. The truth is, I have passed through the schoolgirl crush stage. I have grown, matured, in the last month, in case you haven't noticed. The truth is, Don Champion means absolutely nothing to—"

"He thinks you're a knockout."

"*He does?*" I gasped as Shel pushed past me and went down the stairs. I took off after him. "Don said that about *me?*"

"Okay, you two," Mom said, coming out of the living room, "straighten up in there for me, will you? Get rid of the clutter while I tidy up the powder room." She hurried through the hall toward the "powder room," formerly known as the half bath off the kitchen.

In the living room, Shel calmly swept a week's worth of newspapers and magazines off the coffee table and nudged them under the couch with his foot. I followed him around the room, absently picking up articles of clothing as I went. "Okay," I said when he began whistling under his breath, "let's see, what has Mona Lisa said about you? She says you're, oh, just real great and . . ." He gave me a bored look over his shoulder. "She also says you'd make, uhm, she thinks you and she would make a great couple. Yah, now I remember, that's what she said all right." I had a sudden brainstorm. Glancing over my shoulder to make sure no one was around to overhear the whopper of the year, I said, "Mona says she hopes you and she will get married someday."

His eyes bulged. *"Married?* Good God! I'm not even seventeen yet!" He flung himself onto the couch.

"I'm just kidding, Sheldon. Now, this time," I went on sweetly, "you have to keep your end of the bargain. What did Don say about me?"

He looked at me and rolled his eyes disgustedly. "He says . . . he says you look fairly decent all of a sudden. He says he might even ask you out sometime."

I started laughing. "Well, that's big of him!" Then I went out to the kitchen to see what Mom was up to.

Twenty-three

Packy arrived on the dot of seven thirty. I could tell he was nervous too. His Adam's apple kept bobbing up and down. As he turned out of our driveway he cleared his throat and asked, "Like to take a little spin over to Port Chester?"

"Port Chester?"

"Yeah, that's where all the kids go to drink. It's right over the New York state line. Easier to get served there, Ab."

"Oh. Well, I'm not much of a drinker, Pack," I said. "Besides," I added thankfully, "I don't have any proof."

Patting his jacket pocket, he said, "No problem. I borrowed my cousin's license." He whipped a beat-up driver's license out of his pocket and handed it to me. "Better memorize your name and birthday just in case they ask, Ab."

Under the lights of the Connecticut Turnpike I examined the license. "Do you really think I can pass for . . . Annabel Maria Furlano, brown hair, brown eyes, and five foot *seven?*"

"So"—he grinned over at me—"stand on your toes."

We went to a bar called the Stumble Inn. The bouncer looked about ten feet tall and high as a kite. Packy pushed me toward him, and he peered suspiciously at Annabel's license while I tried to look mature and sophisticated on tiptoe. Maybe I succeeded. The giant finally waved me through.

GUILT was written all over Packy's face, however. The

bouncer snatched his fake ID away from him and held it about two inches from his eyes. "All right, kid," he finally said, "when's your birthday?"

"Uhm, ah"—Packy glanced around wildly—"I—uh—April 1, 1969!"

I clapped a hand to my forehead. Packy had just given the man his actual birth date.

Meanwhile the bouncer grinned evilly. He leaned down so he could look Packy in the eye. "Right, kid," he sneered, "and a happy April Fool's Day to you too." Then he grabbed his arm and . . .

The next thing I knew, Packy had wrenched free and gone bombing up a flight of stairs!

The bouncer started after him, bellowing, "*Get that short kid!*" and fifteen people tore up the stairs after my date!

What was I supposed to do now? The only thing I could think of was to go back outside and wait on the sidewalk. So there I was on my first date, freezing to death in front of something called the Stumble Inn . . . when who should come strolling down the street toward me?

My brother and Mona Lisa. They came up to me and stopped. "What are you doing?" asked Sheldon.

I began to explain when someone called my name. I turned to see Don and Crystal crossing the street toward us. "Fancy meeting all of *you* here!" Crystal said.

Shel ignored her. To me, he said, "Answer my question!"

So I told them.

"Jeesh!" said Shel. "Leave it to my sister. So where's this Cowburn kid now?"

I shrugged. "Running around upstairs somewhere?" I asked, meekly, and Mona broke up.

Throwing a protective arm around my shoulders, Don murmured, "Ditch this idiot and come with us, sweetheart. I'll take care of you."

But Crystal suddenly screamed, "Look!" and pointed at a

pair of legs dangling from a second-story window of the Stumble Inn. "Someone's going to jump!"

"No," said I. "I recognize the legs. It's Packy."

We watched as the rest of Packy emerged from the window. He crouched on the ledge for a moment. Meanwhile we could hear yelling coming from inside. Packy glanced down at us and back in the window a few times. He seemed to shrug. Then he did jump, landing on the grass with a thud! Above him several amazed faces popped out the window.

"Well, don't just stand there!" I yelled at Don and Shel, who were staring openmouthed at my date. "Help him!"

Instantly they went into action. Sheldon grabbed one arm and Don the other. They hauled Packy to his feet. "Can you *walk?*" Shel shouted as if Packy was deaf instead of in shock.

"My ankle," he gasped as a bunch of people came pouring out of the Stumble Inn, yelling and waving their arms over their heads. Don and Shel took one look at that crew and, hooking their arms under Packy's legs, took off up the street.

For a split second Mona and Crystal and I stared at one another. Then we slapped our hands over our mouths and followed the boys.

"You sure you're all right?" Shel was asking as we came pounding up. Packy was sitting in the driver's seat of his car, massaging his left ankle.

"Yeah, I think I twisted it, is all," he answered. "I'm pretty sure it would hurt more if I'd broken it. Thanks for getting me out of there, you guys," he added sheepishly.

"That's okay . . . really," Shel said, looking freaked out.

"Man"—Don shook his head—"what is it with these two?" He nodded at me and Packy. "Every time I see them something weird happens."

"Abbey," said Shel, "has a knack for the weird."

Mona asked, "Why did you do something that dumb, Pack? You could've really hurt yourself."

So Packy explained that when he ran upstairs with all of

those people after him, he hid in a linen closet. But they found him and dragged him out of there, so he broke free and whipped into the men's room. But there being no place to hide in *there*, he did the only other thing he could think of —jumped out a window.

Everyone, including Packy, was kind of smiling and shaking their heads over how silly it was, when Don pulled me off to the side.

"Hey," he said softly, his green eyes fixed on mine, "why don't you ditch this dope, seriously? A girl like you can do a lot better than that guy. Come with us."

Now, I'd be a liar if I claimed that Don couldn't make my heart race. But I couldn't ditch Packy Cowburn. Not if Don were Superman himself could I hurt Packy.

Don nudged me. "If you're worried about Crystal and me, forget it. It's nothing deep. She's an old pal, that's all." He winked.

"Thanks anyway," I whispered, "but I came with Packy tonight and I'm going home with him. I happen to like him. In fact, he may be my ideal man."

"Hey, okay." Don put his hands up, palms out. "But I'll tell you one thing, little girl . . ."

"What's that, Don?"

He gave me a gentle, almost pitying smile. "I'll only ask you once. You shoot me down . . . well"—he shrugged, dropping his hands—"that's it, sweetheart. You've missed your chance with Don Champion."

I smiled my most brilliant smile. "Well, I guess this is it, then." Turning around, I walked over to Packy's car and got in.

As we pulled away from the curb, I waved out the window, calling back to the little group in the street, "See you later, sports fans!" I even blew a kiss—such as I imagined Miss America might. Or a movie star.

Twenty-four

We were back in Norwalk by nine o'clock, so Packy suggested we go to a drive-in. I was so nervous that he might make a pass that I could hardly concentrate on the movie.

I finally began to relax as we drove up Silverwood Avenue and the parkway bridge near my house came into view. My first date was almost over and nothing too embarrassing had happened. Packy had made a number of references to jumping out the window, and I knew he'd get a lot of mileage out of the story at school. So I figured I was home free . . . when he suddenly turned the car off the road into a very dark turnaround.

Jesus, Mary, and Joseph. My palms started sweating. Here it comes—your basic make-out session.

"I had a . . . a really good time tonight, Abbey."

"I did, too, Pack. Thanks."

Long silence. Then, "Would you go out with me again sometime?"

"Sure. I'm really not up to the drinking scene though."

"After what happened tonight," he said, "me *neither.*"

I started laughing . . . until I realized his arm was creeping along the back of the seat. "Shouldn't we . . . get going?" I asked. "I mean, my mother said I had to be home by midnight."

"It's only quarter to, Ab." His hand dangled over my shoulder. "Relax, we've got plenty of time."

For what? I asked, silently. Packy was now inching, nonchalantly, toward me. Suddenly the dangling arm clamped around my shoulders and pulled me across the seat. There was an audible *clack!* as his front teeth met mine.

I pulled away to apologize . . . but all that came out was wild laughter. I was completely out of control!

Packy managed a few weak chuckles, but nothing like the sounds *I* was making. Finally I pulled myself together. "I'm sorry, Packy. I just . . . I can't understand how that happened. Nothing like this has ever happened to me before. I just . . ."

I just shut up because Packy's lips were pressed to mine. The kiss went on . . . and *on. How does one break this off?* I thought. *Should* one break this off? I opened one eye . . . and found myself looking directly into one of Packy's.

How romantic.

This broke me up again, only I was practically crying too. This was awful. "Oh, Packy," I sputtered, fighting for control, "you have to believe me. . . . I'm not laughing at you. I'm . . ." I shut my mouth. He had an ultraserious expression on his face. *Now I've done it,* I thought. *I've hurt his feelings for the last time.* "You're the nicest boy I've ever known," I said. "Really, I . . ."

He looked away. "Oh, Abbey, I think you're so . . . I can't even believe a girl like you would go out with me." Then, very gently, he said, "Did I hurt your teeth?"

"Not too bad. They are a few stars buzzing around overhead, but other than that, I'm perfectly . . ."

This time when his lips touched mine, we didn't knock each other out and I managed to keep my eyes shut. Well, I thought as the kiss ended, I'm sixteen years old and finally been kissed . . . correctly.

As Packy started the car, he looked over at me. "Ab? I kind

of get the impression you've never . . . done this before. Have you?" he asked, kindly.

"You mean my technique doesn't exactly send you?"

"That's one of the good things about you, Ab. You can laugh at yourself . . . even if you are a lousy kisser."

"Thanks a bunch, Pack. Really."

Patting my arm tenderly, he said, "Don't worry, I won't tell any of the guys at school about it."

At the breakfast table the next morning Mom said, "Well, Abbey, tell me about your date. Did you have a good time?"

"Uh, yeah." I ignored Sheldon's piercing stare. "We had . . . fun."

"He seems like a very nice person," Mom said. "Very responsible. Where did you and Packy go?"

"Oh . . . nowhere special," I answered just as Shel made a noise that sounded as if he were blowing his nose in his orange juice.

"Mom . . ." Joyce looked suspiciously from me to Shel. "Something's going on, Mom."

"How was your dinner with Mr. Macartney?" I asked, fast.

"It was perfect." She smiled. "You know, kids . . . I really like him a lot."

"Are you going to marry him?" Joyce asked. "Because if you are I want to know now."

Mom reached across the table to pat her hand. "You're jumping the gun a little, don't you think? I've only seen the man a few times."

"He's coming over again this afternoon, isn't he?" Joyce asked.

Mom turned pink. "Yes, but . . ."

Somewhere inside, I went cold. I tuned the rest of Mom's words out as Shel's eyes met mine across the kitchen table.

Suddenly the phone rang. He and I yelled, "*I'll get it!*" and lunged for it.

For once in my life, I beat my twin to it. Giving him a beatific smile, I snatched up the receiver. "Hel-lo."

"May I speak to Abbey, please?" a boy asked.

"Speaking."

"Abbey? Hi, this is Bassett Hunter, remember me?"

"Sure. How are you, Bassett?" Making a quick rat face at Sheldon, I switched the receiver to my other ear and turned my back on him.

"Pretty good," Bassett said. "I wanted to know if maybe you'd like to go to a lacrosse game this afternoon?" His voice rose uncertainly. "But maybe you don't like lacrosse?"

"I'd love to go," I said. "What time will you pick me up?"

Practically the instant I hung up, the phone rang again. "Jeesh," said Sheldon as I slapped his hand out of the way.

"Abbey, it's Louisa Winch calling. How does your schedule look next week? I need a couple of kids to rototill a garden for me, plant it, keep it weeded . . . you know, the works."

"I don't know much about gardening," I said. "Uh, just a minute, Mrs. Winch. Will you hold on, please?" Shel was flapping his hands in my face. "*What?*"

"I can do it! Don't turn the job down, Ab!"

"No problem, Mrs. Winch," I said into the phone, and cleared my throat delicately. "One of my . . . associates will be pleased to do the job."

I had barely sat down at the table when the phone rang a third time. "Holy Moses," Shel muttered under his breath. "Save it," he said to Joyce as she made a move to get up. "It's got to be for Super Teen over here."

"Abbey?" Packy said. "I'm calling to see how your mouth is this morning. Any visible bruises?"

Shuddering at my tinkling laugh, my family got up and left. But when I hung up the phone, I turned to find Shel lounging in the kitchen doorway. I helped myself to a cup of coffee from the pot on the stove and sat down at the table.

"Since when do you drink coffee?"

I shrugged. "Since now, I guess. I've always wanted to."

"So . . ." He sat down across from me and tipped his chair back, eyeing me. "Guys calling you all the time, your own business. Quite a change from the little butt breath we used to know, hunh?"

"Don't you think it's time you stopped calling me by that odious nickname?"

He brought his chair back down with a thump. "I was wondering when you were going to tell me to stop. I guess that's part of our past, isn't it, Ab? Like a lot of things."

Putting my cup down in the saucer, I nodded. Then, I couldn't help it, I grinned at him. "You know something funny?" He shook his head. "Here I've spent all this time wanting to go back to what was, to a simpler time . . . and all of a sudden I realize that some changes are for the better."

"Of course. You kill me, you really do. How could you not know that?"

I shrugged. "Maybe I'm a slow reader," I said, and he snorted with laughter. We sat there silently while I finished my coffee.

Then Shel said, "Better get ready for the next change, Abbey. And this one will be a bomber too."

"What are you talking about?" I asked, knowing perfectly well what he was talking about.

"She's going to get married again—if not to this guy, to someone else. Think you can handle it?" He gave me a challenging smile.

"I don't know, but I don't have to worry about it yet, so I'm not going to."

Still grinning, Sheldon stretched his hand across the table. "Bet ya, Ab. Ten bucks says she's going to remarry . . . and I'll handle it a whole lot better than you will."

"You are so *queer*," I said, disdainfully. "No one *bets* on whether their own mother will remarry. That will be horrendous! That will be a genuine crisis!"

"Chicken, hunh?" He began making soft clucking sounds.

"If there were two birds sitting on a telephone wire, I bet you'd bet on which one would fly away first!" I said, indignantly. He kept clucking.

Finally I sighed, asking, "Do you have to turn *everything* into a contest?"

"Nah." He shook his head. "Only the hard stuff, Ab. Now quit stalling and answer my question—or are you too chicken to put ten bucks on it?"

I regarded his outstretched hand for a moment. Our eyes met. He grinned, giving a particularly aggressive cluck. "Sheldon," said I, reaching across the table, *"you're on."*

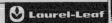 **Laurel-Leaf**

Hung up about growing up? Read
PAULA DANZIGER...
Her hilarious stories about life, love and other hassles will make you laugh out loud!

- [ ] **CAN YOU SUE YOUR PARENTS FOR MALPRACTICE?**   91066-8 $2.75
- [ ] **THE CAT ATE MY GYMSUIT**   91612-7 $2.75
- [ ] **THE DIVORCE EXPRESS**   92062-0 $2.75
- [ ] **IT'S AN AARDVARK-EAT-TURTLE WORLD**   94028-1 $2.50
- [ ] **THE PISTACHIO PRESCRIPTION**   96895-X $2.75
- [ ] **REMEMBER ME TO HAROLD SQUARE**   20153-5 $2.95
- [ ] **THERE'S A BAT IN BUNK FIVE**   98631-1 $2.75
- [ ] **THIS PLACE HAS NO ATMOSPHERE**   98726-1 $2.95

At your local bookstore or use this handy coupon for ordering:

DELL READERS SERVICE, DEPT. DPD
P.O. Box 5057, Des Plaines, IL. 60017-5057

Please send me the above title(s). I am enclosing $_____.
(Please add $2.00 per order to cover shipping and handling.) Send
check or money order—no cash or C.O.D.s please.

Ms./Mrs./Mr._____

Address _____

City/State _____ Zip _____

DPD-1/89

Prices and availability subject to change without notice. Please allow four to six
weeks for delivery. This offer expires 7/89.

Exciting, action-packed adventures by

P.J. PETERSEN

THE BOLL WEEVIL EXPRESS
Three teenagers run away from home, only to find that
the struggle to survive is harder than they thought.

CORKY AND THE BROTHERS COOL
Tim has a great time with Corky, the new guy in town,
until their pranks get them into some deep trouble.

GOING FOR THE BIG ONE
Left on their own, three teenagers camp in the mountains
in search of their father.

HERE'S TO THE SOPHOMORES
It's sophomore year, and Michael is ready for some fast
action—then his best friend becomes the best known and
most controversial guy in school.

NOBODY ELSE CAN WALK IT FOR YOU
A backpacking trip turns into a nightmare when the hikers
are terrorized by a group of motorcyclists.

WOULD YOU SETTLE FOR IMPROBABLE?
When Arnold, teen con artist and delinquent, joins
Michael's ninth grade class, both Arnold and his new
classmates have trouble adjusting to each other.

For a complete listing of these titles, plus many
more, write to us at the address below and we will
send you the Dell Service Listing.

DELL READERS SERVICE LISTING
P.O. Box 1045
South Holland, Illinois 60473

Lose yourself in award-winning teen fiction from

Laurel-Leaf books!

THURSDAY'S CHILDREN
by Rumer Godden

HERE'S LOOKING AT YOU KID
by Jane Breskin Zalben

THE IMPACT ZONE
by Ray Maloney

DOWNWIND
by Louise Moeri

MOTOWN AND DIDI
by Walter Dean Myers

CONFESSIONS OF A WAYWARD PREPPIE
by Stephen Roo

For a complete listing of these titles, plus many more, write to us at the address below and we will send you the Dell Readers Service Listing.

DELL READERS SERVICE LISTING
P.O. Box 1045
South Holland, Illinois 60473

Heart-stopping thrillers by
LOIS DUNCAN
master of mystery and suspense!

DAUGHTERS OF EVE

DOWN A DARK HALL

KILLING MR. GRIFFIN

LOCKED IN TIME

RANSOM

STRANGER WITH MY FACE

SUMMER OF FEAR

THE THIRD EYE

For a complete listing of these titles, plus many more, write to us at the address below and we will send you the Dell Readers Service Listing.

DELL READERS SERVICE LISTING
P.O. Box 1045
South Holland, Illinois 60473

RICHARD PECK

is tuned into teens

ARE YOU IN THE HOUSE ALONE?

CLOSE ENOUGH TO TOUCH

**THE DREADFUL FUTURE
OF BLOSSOM CULP**

DREAMLAND LAKE

THE GHOST BELONGED TO ME

GHOSTS I HAVE BEEN

PRINCESS ASHLEY

REMEMBERING THE GOOD TIMES

REPRESENTING SUPER DOLL

SECRETS OF A SHOPPING MALL

THROUGH A BRIEF DARKNESS

For a complete listing of these titles, plus many more, write to us at the address below and we will send you the Dell Service Listing.

DELL READERS SERVICE LISTING
P.O. Box 1045
South Holland, Illinois 60473

SHOP AT HOME FOR QUALITY BOOKS AND SAVE MONEY, TOO.

Now you can have Dell's Readers Service Listing filled with hundreds of titles, including many books for young adults. Plus, take advantage of our unique and exciting bonus book offer which gives you the opportunity to purchase a Dell book for only 50¢. Here's how!

Just order any five books at the regular price. Then choose any other single book listed (up to a $5.95 value) for just 50¢. Write to us at the address below and we will send you the Dell Readers Service Listing.

**DELL READERS SERVICE LISTING
P.O. Box 1045
South Holland IL 60473**